$10,000,000 Marriage Proposal

JAMES PATTERSON

WITH *HILARY LIFTIN*

BOOK**SHOTS**

13579108642

BookShots
20 Vauxhall Bridge Road
London SW1V 2SA

BookShots is part of the Penguin Random House
group of companies whose addresses can be found at
global.penguinrandomhouse.com

 Penguin
Random House
UK

First published by BookShots in 2016

www.penguin.co.uk

A CIP catalogue record for this book is available from the British Library.

ISBN 9781786530271

Printed and bound in Great Britain by Clays Ltd, St Ives Plc

 MIX
Paper from
responsible sources
FSC® C018179

Penguin Random House is committed to a sustainable future
for our business, our readers and our planet. This book is made
from Forest Stewardship Council® certified paper.

$10,000,000
Marriage
Proposal

CHAPTER 1

IT WAS A Friday morning and Janey Ellis was running late. As usual. She prided herself on being so low maintenance that she could make it from bed to car in twelve minutes flat. The only problem was the getting-out-of-bed part. This morning she could barely drag herself to the shower, having spent the previous evening reading scripts until midnight. Flowerpot Studios had three new TV shows going to series this season, and she was expected to give notes on all of them today—*if* she made it to work in time for her first call.

Sebastian, her ex, used to call her a lane-change demon, and it was true: she would never let some boring gray Prius slow her down. Indeed, she was weaving west on Sunset so fast she would have missed the billboard if it hadn't usurped the one for *her* show. The bright-yellow ad was wrapped around one whole side of a fifteen-story building that until yesterday had promoted the cop drama *Loyal Blue*. *Loyal Blue* was the only successful TV show that Janey had developed to date—the one that looked like it was going to secure her job for the next few years. But it had been cancelled. The finale had aired.

It wasn't her fault. Shows got cancelled all the time, and shows ran for years with worse ratings than *Loyal Blue*. It was a crapshoot. Nonetheless, as Janey's boss had put it, "Money is money and failure is failure." The towering building that had once showcased her success now displayed two-foot-tall Crayola-green letters reading: WILL YOU MARRY ME FOR $10,000,000?

The message was so bold and unexpected that it distracted Janey from wallowing in the sad fate of *Loyal Blue*. This was quite a departure from the TV ads that rotated through this prime Hollywood ad real estate. Janey slowed to gawk. It had to be another reality dating show, right? She cursed herself for not having been the one to come up with it. But then she read the rest of the sign: CREATIVE, OPEN-MINDED BUSINESSMAN WITH LIMITED TIME AND DESIRE TO PLAY THE FIELD. THIS IS A SERIOUS PROPOSAL.

Janey chuckled to herself. It was just weird enough to be legit. Dude obviously had some cash—she'd seen the budget line for the lease on that billboard, and it wasn't cheap. Cars started to honk, and Janey realized the light in front of her was green. She hit the gas a bit harder than she meant to and hurtled through the intersection.

The billboard vanished from Janey's mind as she dashed across the studio lot and hurried into the Flowerpot offices, but not for long. Inside she was a bit surprised to see that everyone—executives and assistants alike—was gathered in her boss's office. Uh-oh. This couldn't be good. After dropping her bag in her office, Janey went to see what was going on.

The roomful of people was staring out the window. "You can see the back of the building, over to the right," an assistant was saying.

"Check out the gridlock," someone else said.

"What's going on?" Janey whispered to her assistant, Elody.

"It's an ad," Elody said. "A ten-million-dollar marriage proposal. It went up this morning and has already gone viral. Gawker says it's caused three fender benders so far."

"I saw it on my way in," Janey said, feeling briefly proud that, for once, she hadn't been the one in the fender bender. "It's got to be some kind of hoax."

"Or a publicity stunt," her colleague Marco said. "Some wannabe actor decided to go big or go home."

"I think it's romantic," Elody said.

A voice boomed over the rest of them. "It's a waste of time and money. This isn't a watercooler, people. It's my office. Out."

Inwardly Janey kicked herself at her mistake. Her boss, J. Ferris White, had been known to can people for taking lunch breaks. Not long lunch breaks. Any lunch break at all. And after the collapse of *Loyal Blue* she needed to get back on his good side. She ducked out of the office with everyone else, feeling twelve years old.

CHAPTER 2

AT 11:00 A.M. on the dot Suze Lee allowed herself her first coffee break of the day. Redfield Partners, though a small venture capital group based in LA, prided itself on offering all the benefits of a big Silicon Valley tech company. Pool and Ping-Pong tables, a half court for basketball, a fully stocked kitchen. The free coffee was supposed to stimulate them to work longer and later, but Suze was pretty sure the excuse for frequent breaks had cut her colleagues' productivity in half. She therefore limited herself to two visits to the café every day, twenty minutes each. Just coffee, no snacking. Today something was different. The café was strangely quiet. The persistent ping-pong of the game that never seemed to cease was silent for once. Instead there was a cluster of people around one of the café tables, where Kevin sat with his laptop.

"I'm sure the guy is sixty years old and ugly as a dog, looking for arm candy," Emily said.

"No! People in the comments are saying that he's a tech billion-aire. Too busy to waste time dating," Kevin said. "I mean, for all we know, he's upstairs now, watching the Tweets roll in." The second floor of Redfield Partners was home to the executive suites, where the investing and operations teams of the firm had their offices (open concept, of course, but still a floor above everyone else). There they met with eager start-ups, counted their millions, and worked out daily in the on-site gym. It was easy to fit it all in when you knew you were set for life. Suze, Kevin, the ten other "entrepreneurs in residence," and the support staff were always encouraged to use the gym, but none of them ever did. Who wanted the hyperfit, life-balance-obsessed partners to see them panting on a treadmill at a slow jog? Instead they took ownership of the in-house café, some of them subsisting solely on its PowerBars and caffeinated beverages.

"Suze—you should totally apply," Meredith said.

Suze practically spat out her iced coffee. "What are you talking about? Why me?"

"Don't play dumb," Meredith said. "I have walked down the street with you. Every man we pass drools, and those are the ones who don't even know that you're brilliant."

"And you're nice. Mostly. A little uptight, but in a nice way," Kevin chimed in.

"Thanks?" said Suze.

"You're the hottest catch in LA," said Jeff.

There was an awkward silence. Jeff, the office IT guy, rarely spoke. When he did, it was always a little creepy.

"He's right," Meredith finally said. "A ten-million-dollar catch."

Suze rolled her eyes. "If that were true…wouldn't I have been caught by now?"

"For ten million dollars you might as well find out," said Kevin.

CHAPTER 3

"CAROLINE! WHERE *ARE* YOU?"

Caroline Fried-Miller cringed. This was working out worse than she'd expected. She'd been living back at home for only two weeks, and already every word out of her mother's mouth got on her nerves. It was not a large house. And yet her mother had to bellow from downstairs as if they'd been separated at an oversold general-admission concert. At this rate Caroline would never last long enough to get back on her feet. Losing her apartment had been an unexpected blow. It was nobody's fault. It had been her roommate Angie's apartment first. Angie had landed the sweet, low-rent beach pad in Venice through a family friend. The lease was in her name. She paid all the bills, and Caroline reimbursed her. That was why it was totally cool when Angie's boyfriend, Bill, started living with them. It was fun, sort of like a super-crowded sitcom. But Caroline should have seen the writing on the wall. When Angie got engaged to Bill (Caroline was so happy for them! She really was!), of course they wanted Caroline out.

Finding a new place on her nonprofit salary wasn't going to be easy. She needed a second job, or something. Meanwhile, stuck at home with her mom and little sister, she was determined to keep the peace. The indomitable Isabelle Fried wasn't going to change. And Caroline was in no position to complain. She rolled out of bed.

"Be right there," she said politely, but at a proper volume that quite possibly would not reach all the way downstairs to her mother. Caroline was willing to be respectful, but that didn't mean she had to compromise her standards. She refused to turn into her mother.

"Hurry, look, you'll miss it!" her mother urged as Caroline came into the living room. "This is it, honey, your golden ticket!"

Isabelle was staring at the TV, where the local news was covering a story Caroline had glimpsed on her phone on the way downstairs. Something about a billboard with a marriage proposal.

"Mom, I am not Cinderella. Please don't fairy-godmother me."

"Don't be such a snob. It's fun. This man, whoever he is, is obviously smart, or he wouldn't be rich, and he's obviously determined, or he wouldn't be launching this impressive campaign. He knows what he wants and he's willing to pay for it. You should try out, honey. You've got nothing to lose!"

"Um…thank you for thinking of me, but I'm not for sale."

Isabelle shook her head. "Don't be obstinate. He's not buying *you*. He's buying opportunity."

Caroline laughed. "Okay, you win."

"So you'll do it. Great. The audition is tomorrow—"

"What? No!" Caroline shook her head. "You win that he's *buying opportunity*. You don't win entering me into the wife contest."

"Are you sure?" her mother asked. "You know, you haven't had a boyfriend since He Who Shall Not Be Mentioned. It's not like you have a good track record with finding your own boyfriends. Might as well put it in the hands of fate."

"Yeah. No."

Isabelle stared at her daughter. Then she got a glint in her eye. "Five hundred dollars," she said. "I'll give you five hundred dollars."

"Uh, Mom? I'm not an idiot. If I won't do it for ten million dollars, why would I do it for five hundred?"

"Because I'll give you the five hundred just for trying."

"Do I get five hundred dollars, too?" Caroline's little sister, Brooke, piped in from the doorway.

"Get ready for school, sweetie," Isabelle told her second daughter.

Caroline said, "How about you give me five hundred dollars to clean out the garage, which I've been doing in my spare time for two weeks now? Isn't that worth five hundred dollars?" She could really use the money. When she moved out, a landlord was going to ask for first month's rent and a month's deposit—cash she didn't have sitting around.

"Five hundred dollars to take a chance with Prince Charming. Deal or no deal?" her mother said.

"No deal." Caroline couldn't be bought by a man, and she certainly didn't want to be bought by her mother.

"I'll do it for two hundred!" Brooke said.

"Get your backpack, we're late," Isabelle told Brooke.

CHAPTER 4

THREE DAYS LATER Caroline was navigating to the downtown address her mother had given her. Her laptop battery had died its last death three hours after their conversation about the contest. Between the shame of borrowing her sister's babysitting savings to help pay for a new computer and the shame of auditioning for the role of a rich man's wife, she had opted for the latter, and now here she was.

As she drove south on Figueroa Street, there were no big office buildings, nothing that looked like a place where a man could interview several potential wives. Nothing…except the Staples Center.

"You have arrived at your destination: 1111 South Figueroa Street."

"You have got to be kidding me," Caroline said out loud. The goddamn Staples Center. She couldn't help but laugh. This was so absurd that it might actually be worth it.

It was a cattle call. If it had been anywhere other than LA, Caroline would have assumed she'd walked into some kind of pageant or convention for models, or into any gym in LA, where you'd find a high ratio of sculpted bodies, chemically colored and straightened blond hair, and obscenely long eyelash extensions. Caroline instinctively reached to her own hair. It had been honey blond when she was a kid, but now the best she could do was to beg her colorist to try to replicate the color she'd once had naturally. When she could afford it. Which, as anyone who saw her roots would know, was about six months ago.

The women were lining up by last name. Caroline found *A–F* and took her place at the back. The tall, skinny blond woman in front of her caught her eye and smiled.

"Hey—don't I know you?" she asked.

"I don't think so?" Caroline peered at her. She looked familiar, but only in that LA way—she was either a regular at Caroline's neighborhood Starbucks or a bit actor on *Law & Order.* Both were a dime a dozen.

"No, I know why I recognize you," the woman insisted. "As kids we went to all the same auditions. You looked as miserable as I felt. But I didn't last long—I quit acting in high school."

"At least you quit. That makes you smarter than I was. I failed my way out," Caroline said.

"Well, I quit to model, so…maybe not." They both laughed. But suddenly Caroline realized what she had gotten herself into. This *again.* Her mother had been doing this to her since she was a kid—putting her up for singing contests, auditions, talent searches. Isabelle Fried needed her oldest daughter to be a star. Thankfully, Brooke was exempt. She had fallen in love with piano at age three and was a borderline prodigy. Apparently, that was enough for Isabelle. But Caroline was not so lucky. Her entire childhood had been a relentless exercise in rejection, loss, failure. And yet here she was, twenty-six, still somehow suckered into living out someone else's dream. It was starting to say more about her than it was about her mother.

She looked around the room: at the generic but friendly model who was still talking to her, and the sea of hopeful women left and right, all looking for a shortcut, all trying to win a lottery against terrible odds. The last thing Caroline wanted or needed was one more affirmation that she was not as desirable as everyone else.

"Good luck to you," she told the blond woman. "I think this time I'm the one who should be quitting."

And with that, Caroline marched out of the automatic glass doors.

CHAPTER 5

SUZE TOOK A seat at the end of a row and scanned the questionnaire she'd been handed. It was six pages long and reminded her of the online dating profiles she'd helped friends create now and then. The top of the form had a number of basic questions about her appearance, educational background, religion, and lifestyle. Then came the more open-ended, philosophical questions. There had to be a strategy to these self-profiles, Suze supposed, some clever way to answer these questions that would make her stand out from the rest and at the same time maximize her chances of appealing to the bachelor in question. But she had never been one to play games. If you tricked someone into picking you, then you had to keep up the act indefinitely. False advertising was for people with low self-esteem.

Suze carefully assessed the personal information required. It was minimal and safe. Even if this was one big joke, at least it wasn't an identity theft scam. After filling in the short answers by hand, she came to the first open-ended question: *Why are you here today?* She took out her handheld thermal printer (the Zoom, one of Redfield's most promising ventures) and began to type. *In my job at a venture capital firm, I offer innovators large sums of money to support great ideas. So if this offer is made in the spirit of finding true love, I respect the idea of using money to do it. We use money to find everything else....*

The questions were increasingly probing, but they made sense to Suze. With all these candidates, how could the millionaire possibly choose one person out of the crowd? *What do you like to do on weekend nights? Tell me about your ambitions. What is your perfect first date?* On it went. Suze was glad for her Zoom. It allowed her to self-edit as she went, then print out her paragraphs as neat labels to affix to the questionnaire. She made a mental note to recommend that the partners boost their investment in the next round.

The final question was the first one she had never had cause to answer before: *Are you here for love or money?*

I am here out of curiosity, she wrote. *I understand that my chances of walking away with either love or money are low. It's not that I'm a pessimist, but the odds are simply against it. However, if I did find love, or what promised to be a very high chance of true love, I would be willing to leave the money on the table.* She leaned back to consider what she'd written before she printed it out. It was a logical answer. She imagined being happily married, and being offered ten million dollars to leave her husband. She would never do such a thing; therefore, love trumped money. Of course, it was hard to imagine feeling that way about a man she hadn't yet met, but a hypothetical scenario could only have a hypothetical response. She hit Print, affixed the final label neatly to the questionnaire, and brought it back to the intake desk.

"Thank you," the woman at the desk said. She scanned the application.

"Most of the applicants didn't even bring something to write with. But you seem to have...what are these, labels?"

Suze smiled. "I love my gadgets."

The woman smiled back at her. "Cool," she said. Then she beckoned Suze closer conspiratorially. "You also happen to be one of the most beautiful women here. Remember to smile. You have a nice one, and he likes a smile. Good luck."

"Thank you," Suze said. She stood for a moment, hoping the woman might elaborate, but she was already calling the next applicant. Suze had been dismissed. *He likes a smile.* It wasn't much, but it was all she was going to get. Well, at least it meant there was an actual human being somewhere behind this crazy scheme.

CHAPTER 6

THIS MONDAY MORNING Janey Ellis had no excuse for her tardiness. Her alarm had been functioning, but, damnit, the clock itself seemed to be moving faster than usual. That, or she was reluctant to face what awaited her at work. Two weeks of pitching new potential TV shows to cable stations had just concluded, and what did she have to show for it? Nothing. Not a single nibble. And this was following an equally dismal reception by networks. She'd worked like a dog to help her writers repurpose their pitches for cable—edgier, with antiheroes and preferably some form of sex that nobody had done yet (which was increasingly difficult to find). She'd never been in this position before. Entering pilot season with no shows to develop was grim. She'd be a team player—working her ass off to help out her colleagues on the two shows that Flowerpot had successfully sold—but the glory would be all theirs.

Stuck at the stoplight on the corner of Sunset and Crescent Heights, she saw it again. That ridiculous billboard. A lottery of love. People were truly starting to live their lives as if they were reality shows. Next thing you knew, people would be taking *Survivor*-themed vacations—forty days on a deserted island just for kicks and weight loss. Janey found herself wondering if the ten-million-dollar bachelor had a producer yet—but only for a minute. This was Hollywood. Of course he already had a producer. If he didn't, he was a truly rare breed: rich and naive.

It seemed like a normal Monday. There was no sign of impending doom. Even in hindsight Janey would say that the office had its usual bustle. No funny looks or sympathetic smiles. She had just made her coffee when J. Ferris asked her into his office. He shut the door behind them. That was arguably a clue, but it came only seconds before the ax.

"You had a bad season, Janey." J. Ferris sat down at his desk, but he didn't gesture for Janey to take a seat. She stood behind one of his guest chairs, noting that he had nothing personal on his desk. No photos, no desk toys, nothing with any color whatsoever. The guy was married and had at least two kids. Or was it three?

"I know I did. We really had some strong pitches, but I think—"

"We're not here to quarterback it. I'm letting you go." He hit the space bar on his keyboard to wake it up, seemed to glance at his new e-mails, then looked back at Janey. She was pretty confident he had no idea he'd actually just checked his e-mail in the middle of firing her, but it was offensive nonetheless.

"What? Please don't do that—I mean, I'm so committed to—"

"The job is to sell pilots. You failed. You're not earning your keep. This isn't summer camp. This is a business. You're a loss. It's that simple."

"Okay," Janey said. "I mean, I'm really surprised. Every studio has ups and downs, and—"

"And people lose their jobs for it." He nodded to the doorway. A security guard had appeared. "Collect your personal items. We give fifteen minutes. It's not that we don't trust you." He stood up. "It's just what we do here."

"Good-bye. Thank you for the opportunity." What else was she supposed to say? As far as she could tell, J. Ferris was barely human. "This company really shouldn't have been called Flowerpot Studios," she muttered under her breath as she returned to her office. "It sounded like such a warm, homey place and it's just *not*." The security guard came to attention, as if he thought Janey might go postal. Janey stopped muttering and hurriedly threw anything personal into file boxes. But she couldn't bring herself to leave like this. Before the security guard could stop her, she walked back into J. Ferris's office without knocking. He looked up.

"You are a cold, selfish person. It might be good for business, but it's not good for life. Here's a piece of advice. Bring in some photos of your family. Maybe say hi to people when you walk past them in the hall. It won't kill you." Janey walked out of the office before he could respond. She turned to the security guard, who was following her, and said, "You're probably going to get in trouble for that, so I'm sorry, but it had to be done."

Ten minutes later she was in her car, breaking the news to her assistant.

"I'm so sorry—I have no idea what will happen to you. I had

no warning whatsoever, but as soon as I find another job, I'll try to bring you in."

"It's okay," Elody said. "Don't worry about me. They already re-assigned me. I'll be working with Marco."

"Oh. Wow. Great." That was fast. "I'm so relieved it's just me." But as the words "just me" came out of her mouth, Janey felt hot tears spring to her eyes. "I'd better let you get to it, then!" she said as brightly as she could, and got off the phone before she embarrassed herself. Yeah, it had been a bad match, or whatever she was supposed to tell herself. But she felt like she'd been sucker punched. Now what was she going to do? It was 10:45 on a Monday morning, and she had no place to go. She pulled into the valet for the Tower Bar. She'd never had a cocktail in the morning. Now seemed like a perfect time to start.

Waiting for her Bloody Mary to arrive, Janey glanced out the window and saw the billboard for the second time that day. The Tower Bar had a perfect view of it—as if the guy had been sitting right here having a drink when he had the idea. She glanced at the bartender. Was it him? The mystery bachelor could be anyone. But the scruffy bartender looked like he'd rather be anywhere but here. There was no way that guy had millions of dollars to throw away.

The Bloody Mary, which was her first, tasted much better than she'd expected. As she sipped it, she looked more closely at the poster. There was no TV network mentioned on it anywhere. No logo. Hmmm. Maybe this guy was just eccentric enough not to have sold the rights to his story. She pulled up the website on her phone. Nothing there, either, just information for interested candidates. Apparently, applications were due today. In person. At a downtown address that, as the internet confirmed, was the Staples Center. Oh, this was going to be good. Janey downed half her Bloody Mary (for courage), stopped in the restroom to check that the morning's trauma wasn't written all over her face, and drove downtown with a sense of purpose. A ten-million-dollar marriage proposal. It was a waste of her time, but, as of this morning, she had nothing but time.

CHAPTER 7

CAROLINE TRIED TO be strong, but the five-hundred-dollar carrot that her mother had dangled proved irresistible. She reminded herself that—unlike the umpteen auditions her mother had sent her on—this time the only reward she anticipated was 100 percent guaranteed. This was the very definition of realistic expectations. She had zero chance of rejection or disappointment. On the contrary, she would waste away a morning with a bunch of desperate women in exchange for the funds to buy a brand-new computer. It was a good deal.

Caroline reentered the crowded stadium. Maybe the best way to get through this would be to pretend it was a social experiment. Who were these women? And why were they here? She hadn't sat in her car for long, but somehow there were now twice as many women lining up for applications. Each was dressed in what she, this morning, had presumably deemed a marriage-proposal-winning outfit. Waiting in line, Caroline tried to characterize them. There was a powerful contingent of ladies in formfitting minidresses flaunting their curves with varying degrees of good taste; then there were the standard LA pseudo-Bohemians, a faux-casual tribe of blown-out blondes with expensive jeans and four-inch heels; and, finally, there was a woeful minority of average women in nondescript business casual who appeared to have simply stopped by on their way to work. *What might this room look like if a woman had made the offer?* Caroline found herself musing. *It would be a sea of clueless dudes in generic navy-blue suits,* she thought, and none of them would be penalized for lack of originality.

There must have been nearly two hundred women ahead of her in the line for last names beginning with *A* through *F.* At this rate, she'd be waiting for at least an hour just to get an application. This never happened in fairy tales.

Welcome to the fairy tale from hell.

CHAPTER 8

SUZE HAD MANAGED to be relatively productive for most of the three hours she'd allocated to this farce—huddled in a corner answering e-mails—but just before her timer went off, a male voice came on the PA system.

"Thank you all for your patience," he said warmly. Was it *him?* Was he here, hidden in some security lookout, secretly checking out the candidates?

"While we anticipated a response like this—ten million dollars is a lot of money—" He was interrupted by whoops and cheers from the assembled crowd. "This will require a serious effort. We are trying not to waste your time, so we have already selected a number of you to move to the next stage. Please do not be hurt or offended if you are not called. You are all worthwhile people, but we are keeping one man's taste and personality in mind. We hope you understand. Thank you for your time and courage. Please refer to the numbers on your application receipts." He then began to read numbers, as if announcing the winners of a lottery. There was a rustle of paper as the women pulled out the stubs from their applications, where their numbers appeared in the upper-left corner. Suze's number was 2111, and it came up almost right away. She had a feeling it must have been thanks to that woman who'd advised her to smile. Suze had an ally.

Suze slid upstream through the departing crowd and found herself in a group of about forty women clustered near the application desks.

"This way, please." A woman in a gray suit led them through a door to a conference room. Here they would wait even longer, but at least there were sofas and water bottles. Three separate doors appeared to lead to three different meeting rooms, and it seemed that one of the candidates was called into a room about every twenty minutes. This was it! Suze was about to meet Mr. Moneybags. She checked her makeup in her phone camera. It was fine. She wasn't someone who looked terrible one day and gorgeous the next. Her hair was long and straight, smooth and dark. Her skin had always been flawless. She knew she was lucky not to have to worry. Her friends seemed to pick apart their own faces and bodies, wanting fuller lips, stronger chins, smaller noses, longer legs, and so on. Suze knew she wasn't perfect, but she had never felt compelled to mess with what she had. She just stuck to the same routine. It had worked for her so far.

Although she still didn't feel invested in this unlikely contest, Suze felt an unexpected flutter of excitement when her name was finally called. At last she was going to meet the mysterious millionaire. Would he be physically unappealing? A beast looking for his beauty? Odds were yes. She walked calmly into the room, an interview smile deliberately frozen on her face. But hold on. Instead of the man she expected to find, perhaps smiling sheepishly in a custom-made suit, she found herself in front of two women and a man. A jury.

The man spoke: "Are you"—he looked down at a paper—"Suze Lee?"

"I am," she said.

The women and man smiled at her. "Well, welcome to your interview, Suze. This is going to be straightforward. We'd like to know all about you, but what you choose to tell us is completely up to you. Just please be truthful. Is that fair?"

"That's fair." Suze smiled back. *He likes a smile.* She made sure to keep it there when she spoke. "Technically one-sided, but fair." The three chuckled.

"Okay," one of the women said, "if you don't mind, let's start with your parents. What kind of marriage did Mom and Dad have?"

CHAPTER 9

CAROLINE INSTINCTIVELY SAT straight in the chair, legs crossed at the ankles, knees held tightly together. Interview mode.

"I can see that you're being sincere," one of the women behind the desk was saying, "and I know this is weird and hard to do in such a strange setting, but it would help if you didn't worry about saying the right thing." She was wiry, with sharp features and funky blue glasses. She looked smart.

"Yeah," the other woman said. She was pretty, in a less funky, more natural way. Blond hair, no makeup, and a cotton fisherman sweater—straight out of an Ivory soap commercial. "Try to imagine you've known us for years. Because remember what we're doing here. We're not looking for someone who's good at playing the role of wife. We're actually looking for a genuine connection—or at least the potential for one."

The sole male interviewer was young and magazine handsome, with charmingly tousled dark hair and a mischievous glint in his eyes. If he didn't turn out to be Prince Charming, he was a good choice for an interviewer, Caroline thought. The women, too.

They were all so friendly and attractive that there was a subtle psychological suggestion that the would-be husband would not prove to be a toad.

"I get it," Caroline said. "And I have to admit that's a relief. I'm done with acting—on stage or in real life. But I will keep trying to sit up straight, if that's okay by you. It's false advertising, I confess, but I might as well stick with it as long as I can."

The Ivory soap girl made an obvious point of fixing her own posture, and the one with blue glasses followed suit.

"Much better, ladies," Caroline said. "Strong cores all around."

The group laughed.

"So, let's hear about what brought you here today," the male interviewer said.

"You want the truth? Five hundred dollars," Caroline said.

"Uh, not to focus on the monetary aspect, but you do know it's ten million, right?" the woman in blue glasses said.

"Sure, I know. But my mother bribed me to come here. I was…incentivized. Still, I'm open to finding love. And an apartment. Possibly a higher-paying job, except I love what I do. I definitely need to get out of my mother's house! Gosh, I sound like a basket case, don't I? But I'm actually not.…"

"We know that life has ups and downs," said Ivory Girl. "We're not looking for perfection."

"Seriously? Because for ten million dollars I would want perfection," Caroline said. Then she paused. It wasn't really true. She didn't want Mr. Perfect and never had. She wanted someone quirky and unpredictable. She didn't have everything figured out, and she wanted to carve out a life with someone. In fact, now that she thought about it, that was why she couldn't really take this contest seriously. Anyone who had all that money to spend, and all these women to choose from…his life had to be more established than hers. She didn't want to be the last piece in someone else's life puzzle. She started to stand up. "You guys seem cool. I don't want to waste your time. I can just—"

"Hold on a minute," the guy said. "I'm curious about what just went through your mind. What made you want to bolt?"

"It's just—I would never step into the 'wife' vacancy in someone's otherwise complete life. I'm sure this guy—*whoever he is…*" And here she gave the male interviewer a pointed stare and paused. With an amused look on his face, he shook his head with a nearly imperceptible *no*. Caroline went on. "This guy has it all down. His life is on a track, and he wants a companion to take the ride with him. Totally makes sense. I wish him happiness. But I'm not that girl."

"Well, that's refreshing," the woman in the blue glasses said.

"And certainly not disqualifying," the Ivory girl reassured her.

"Please stay," the guy said. "We want to hear more."

And so Caroline told them about her ill-paying but beloved job as a social worker for incarcerated youth. She made them laugh with her best stories about her crazy stage mom ("World's Worst Mother-in-Law. Don't say I didn't warn him"). And, since she was on a roll, she rattled off a list of pros and cons about her candidacy: great cook, though only for guests; loves animals except reptiles; closet Belieber; tries anything once; hates theater; bites nails in public; has trouble staying up past ten o'clock and always falls asleep in movies; has forgotten everything from art and history classes; cannot deal with spiders.

Caroline knew she was not a "catch," if there was such a thing, but the interviewers made her feel as comfortable as was conceivable, considering she was talking about herself the whole time. It was only when they started to wrap up that Caroline realized a full hour and a half had passed. She'd been to enough auditions to know that the amount of time they gave you was a sure indicator of how well you'd done. Apparently, she was rocking this interview!

The guy interviewer looked at his watch, then directly at her. "It's been fun talking to you, Caroline. You obviously don't hold back."

"Sorry!" Caroline said, covering her face with her hands. "I'm such a blabbermouth."

"We just need to ask you if there's anything else we should know," Blue Glasses said.

There was something. Caroline hadn't spoken of it to anyone—not in detail. But there was something about these people… maybe it was a ploy, but they made her feel like the more she exposed, the more likeable she was.

"Well, this has been the best therapy session of my life, thank you very much," Caroline said. "I might as well tell you everything. But this is kind of the worst." She took a deep breath. "Ten months ago my boyfriend broke it off—it wasn't just that he ended things, it was the way it happened. I've never been so humiliated. He isn't a bad person. I'm sure it must have been at least partly my fault. But the whole thing was especially bad because…" She felt a heat rising up her face, and she was getting a little choked up. She stopped.

"It's okay, don't feel like you have to say more. That sounds really hard," said Ivory with real sympathy in her voice. Blue Glasses said nothing, but she nodded in agreement, and she even seemed to have tears in her eyes. Wow, these people were genuinely kind. Why? Where had they come from? What was this all about?

CHAPTER 10

"I LOST MY job this morning. Literally. I'm on the rebound, so watch out." All three of the interviewers laughed.

"So tell us your story," the woman in the blue glasses said. "A bit about who you are and what brought you here—aside from the job breakup, that is."

"Who is Janey Ellis?" Janey joked. "Okay, here goes. I grew up in a little town outside Iowa City. You've never heard of it, and that's why I'm not there anymore. Except at Christmas, which is ridiculously adorable. You guys have no idea. Anyway, I'm a TV producer, which I'm really good at and love even though I got fired this morning. So…consider me unappreciated but good. And make no mistake—I'll have a couple job offers by the end of the week.

"But let me ask you something. It seems obvious to me that your boss, Mystery Man, is a reality show waiting to happen, and I'm wondering if you've already made a deal for it. In any case, you should hire me! I can pitch on that, if you like. But I also want to say that at the exact same time, I am not-so-secretly hoping to be plucked from obscurity and anointed Mrs. Mystery Man. I'm not proud! I would go on a blind date for zero dollars, so ten million is totally in my ballpark.

"Whew, I had too much coffee today. After the Bloody Mary. Which I had only because I got fired. I swear to you it's the first time I've ever had a morning cocktail, and I don't plan to make it a habit. Unless I'm engaged by the end of today, in which case, why stop?"

Her interviewers had been surprisingly alert when she came in, considering they must have been listening to life story after life story, but Janey was giving them her A game, and now they were laughing. If there was one thing Janey was good at, it was charming a roomful of executives. She could pitch herself as well as any TV show.

"Well, Janey, you obviously have a lot to offer. If you don't mind my asking, why are you single?" the cute guy interviewer asked.

"Long answer or short answer? The long answer has all kinds of details about dating the wrong men for the right reasons and how I am too quick to trust people. It has something to do with Iowa and my parents, who are best friends and never fight. And the shorter answer is that I left my last boyfriend. He cheated on me. Twice. As far as I know." Janey thought about Sebastian, that bastard. He'd been a hard one to let go. She'd had to delete him from her phone, purge his e-mails, and remove every reminder of him from her house lest she relapse. But now, for her audience, she laughed. "Fool me once, shame on you. Fool me twice, shame on me. Honestly, if finding true love were my only goal, I would go straight back to Iowa. It's pretty nice there, and you can take people at face value."

CHAPTER 11

SUZE DIDN'T SLIP back into the office until after two, hoping against hope that her colleagues wouldn't notice, or remember what she'd been up to this morning. As if. She hadn't even pulled out her laptop when Meredith was already in one of her visitor chairs, tapping her fingers impatiently.

"Download please. Tell me everything."

"It's nothing, really. I just—"

Before Suze could continue, Kevin, Emily, and Jeff filed into the office, as if appearing for a scheduled meeting.

"Go back to the beginning," Emily said.

"You guys! I have nothing to report! Will you get off my case?" Suze protested.

Meredith looked at her watch. "Five hours of nothing? Please. We know you. You've never let five hours go by with nothing to show for it," Meredith said. "What was he like? How old? Handsome? Are you sure he's for real?"

"Fine. I met him. He is about my age, around thirty. Very handsome—like a young George Clooney...." If they were going to be nosy, she'd give them exactly what they wanted. Suze dropped her voice down to a whisper, so that her friends leaned closer to her. "He told me that he had three questions, and that if I answered them to his satisfaction, he would ask me to marry him and hand me a check for ten million dollars."

"So much pressure!" Meredith exclaimed.

Suze was getting into her tale. "I'll admit, I was nervous. But I told myself that all I could do was answer the questions honestly and to the best of my ability, and if that wasn't sufficient, so be it. Calmly and politely he asked the first question. It was a simple one. Just 'Where are you from?' That was easy, of course."

"You're from Boston, right?" Kevin asked.

"Right. And then he asked what my favorite hobbies and interests are outside work. I told him about running the marathon, how I love to play the piano but don't own one, and how when I was a kid, I was kind of a golf prodigy. And I told him I've always wanted to learn to fly-fish."

"Fly-fishing, that's brilliant!" said Emily.

"Genius," said Kevin.

"It happens to be true," said Suze.

"What was the third question?" Jeff asked. "It's always the third question that matters."

"You're right, Jeff," Suze said. "The third question was…" She paused for dramatic effect. "The third question was, 'Why are your office mates so up in your business?'" There was a moment of silence as they all realized she'd made up the whole thing.

"You didn't even meet him, did you?" said Jeff.

"Nope," Suze said. "Now will you let me get back to work?"

"So that's it? You're out?" Meredith said. "I can't believe it. Did you get to see who he picked?"

Suze's pride prickled at the assumption that she hadn't been chosen. "Actually, I think I'm still in the running. The finals, or whatever. I was invited to go to his home this Sunday."

"Holy moly!" said Meredith. "That's huge. You could win this! Ten million dollars! Oh, my God." Then, looking at Suze urgently, she said, "You have to go. You're going, aren't you?"

CHAPTER 12

CAROLINE FELT WIRED when she left the interview. It had been unexpectedly fun—like a date that had gone particularly well. There was a sense of hope and anticipation. What would come next? Her enthusiasm was only slightly dampened by her mother. She had barely put the car in Park when Isabelle and Brooke surged from the house into the driveway, demanding to know what had happened.

"You were gone all day!" Brooke said. "Did you win?"

"No, sweetie," Caroline said.

"What? That's ridiculous," Brooke said.

Her mother scowled in disappointment. "Who did they pick? Did you even have a chance to sing?" Isabelle pursed her lips. "It's not that you're lacking, Caroline. It's that you don't *sell* yourself. Did they give you a contact number? I would like to call—don't worry, sweetie, I won't embarrass you, but they do owe you an explanation."

"Mom, there were, like, two thousand other women there. They don't owe me anything."

"You always did give up too easily. You have to fight for what you want. Haven't I taught you anything?"

"Can you please just tell us what happened?" Brooke asked.

"If you let me get out of my car," Caroline said.

She was starving. She started fixing herself a turkey sandwich and filled in her mother and sister on the strange, strange day.

"Like I said, there were lots and lots of women there."

"Leggy blondes?" her mother said. "If that's what he wants, then good riddance."

"Exactly what you'd expect. But I was among a group of about forty who were asked to interview."

Isabelle's face immediately transformed, her eyes now bright with expectation. "You did it, baby! You got called back! I knew you could do it if you really, really wanted it. I've always said that if you just set your mind to success—and maybe had a little work done—"

"So when is the callback?" Brooke asked.

"Actually, they already interviewed me, so it might be over already. They didn't say anything about another meeting. I don't really know where I stand."

"Jerks," Brooke said.

"No, actually, that's the weird part. The interviewers were shockingly normal. They seemed to really care about who I was as a person, not just what I looked like or whether I'd make an ideal wife. They were—I don't know—*likeable,* even after conducting who knows how many interviews. Prince Charming, whoever he is, has good taste in people. It made me kind of curious about him."

"If he has such good taste in people, how come he can't find his own girlfriend all by himself?" Brooke asked.

"Good point," Caroline said.

"Is there a contact number?" Isabelle said. "We really should follow up. I'm going to check in. Find out your standing."

"Mom, please don't," Caroline said.

"No, Mom," Brooke said at the same time.

Isabelle pursed her lips in frustration. "I'm not going to just sit around and wait."

"That makes three of us," said Caroline.

CHAPTER 13

THE MEETING WAS set for 10:00 p.m. Suze was uncomfortable with the timing. Why so late? What made this a safe situation? She'd signed a nondisclosure that required her to keep every element of this meeting private, but she wasn't an idiot. She put Meredith on call. The deal was, if Meredith didn't get a text from Suze by midnight, she was authorized to open the fingerprint-locked e-mail Suze had sent her with all the confidential information. Thanks to a technology Redfield had invested in, Suze would then receive an automatically generated text. If something went amiss, not only would Meredith have the mystery man's address in hand but Suze could use the autotext as proof to him that the police were en route. She was certainly curious enough at this point to agree to a meeting at a Bel Air mansion late at night, but she wasn't taking any chances.

The car dropped Suze off at the end of a long, gated drive. There was a cobblestoned cul-de-sac, well lit, with two architectural olive trees in the center. The house was sprawling but traditional, with nothing showy or oversized. An understated mansion. The entrance was warmly lit, making the late hour less creepy, and the wide front porch had powder-blue Adirondack chairs on it, a bit askew, as if someone actually made use of them. Suze noticed, as she rang the doorbell, how utterly quiet everything was. There was no traffic up here in the hills. No neighboring houses within sight. No sign of any other finalists. She nearly double-checked the address, but the millionaire's car had brought her here. It had to be the place. Maybe everyone was out back. Or maybe she was here alone. Or maybe this was a test and she was being watched right now. She reflexively reached into her bag to touch her phone. It was her safety line, one that would work even if she couldn't access it.

A woman in blue glasses opened the door. "Suze! Welcome. I'm sorry it took me so long to get to the door. This place is big! Frankly, I'm a little winded after walking from the library." She ushered Suze in. "By the way, my name is Alicia. Congratulations on making it to this stage." *This stage,* Suze noted. She hadn't won yet.

As she talked, Alicia led Suze to the left, down a wide hallway. They passed a large formal living room with a wall of sliders opening out onto a well-lit backyard. There was a dining room with an obscenely long table and several paintings that certainly belonged in a museum. They turned again, into another wing—the house seemed to be U-shaped, with a courtyard in the middle. The rooms along this hallway were clearly more lived in: First there was a comfortable game room with a pool table, bar, and a few retro pinball machines. Then they came to a library with floor-to-ceiling built-in bookshelves, overstuffed reading chairs, and a wide antique desk.

"Please have a seat here," Alicia said, directing her to one of the chairs. "What can I get you to drink? A glass of wine? Coffee or tea? Water? Whatever you want."

"Just water is fine, thanks," Suze said, then thought better of it. This wasn't a business meeting! It was a date—or if all went well, it might turn into one. "On second thought, a glass of red wine would be perfect."

"You got it," Alicia said. "And don't worry if it takes me a little while—the kitchen is at least a mile away."

Suze waited. This had to be Mr. Moneybags' house, right? It certainly fit the bill. Was he lurking here somewhere? Scared to meet her, or just biding his time? She looked around. Was she being observed? Filmed? She stood up and started looking at the books that lined the shelves, pulling out one on Renaissance art. Might as well learn something while she waited. Plus, not to be calculating, but it didn't hurt to clue him in the minute he entered that she was no bimbo.

CHAPTER 14

ANOTHER WOMAN CAME into the library—Suze recognized her as the woman from the Staples Center who had counseled her to smile at Mr. Moneybags, as if that opportunity would actually someday arrive. Apparently, it now had.

"I'm sorry," she said. "Alicia had to step away. But I brought you your wine." The woman lowered the shades on the sliders. "Here, this is cozier, isn't it?"

Suze had a thousand questions she wanted to ask, but she sensed she hadn't gotten far enough to earn that. When entrepreneurs came to Redfield seeking funding, they were expected to make their case, presenting all the information in a coherent and convincing way before Redfield gave them any indication of interest or partnership. Suze knew where she stood. But that didn't mean it wasn't worth a shot.

"How many of us are there at this point?" she whispered to her presumed ally.

"It's not a competition," the woman said. "Not in the traditional sense. He's not comparing women. He's just looking for one.

The one. It'll just be a moment. Good luck. And don't be nervous—just be yourself."

Easy for you to say, Suze thought. But the wine was an excellent idea. A few sips in, Suze's doubts and mild paranoia fled, and she was left to appreciate the luxurious setting and romantic scenario in which she found herself. This was a real-life fairy tale. Somewhere out there was a man. Would he sweep her off her feet? Did she even believe in love at first sight? He seemed to have confidence in this process—otherwise, how could he trust that from it his perfect mate would emerge? She herself had a mental list of what she wanted in a man, but she wasn't wed to it. There had to be variables; anyone with half a brain knew that.

Suddenly, without fanfare, a man dressed casually in jeans, loafers, and a pullover came out and sat down across from her. He was in his midthirties, handsome, with a warm smile. Suze felt an unfamiliar combination of relief and disappointment. Here he was at last—the man who had sparked all this drama and speculation, the owner of this dream estate, a person who was willing to spend anything on his search for the right woman. He was certainly more than attractive enough, but now that he was in front of her, Suze felt a vague sense of loss. Gone was the magic of not knowing anything. The mystery of a man who had no features and no form. The unknown had been more intriguing than this real person sitting before her. Suze instantly saw it as a flaw in the process—he'd built himself up to be a god and then exposed himself as a mere mortal.

"I'm Brendan," he said. "You must be Suze." He looked down

at a piece of paper. "I know a lot about you from this, but is it okay if I ask a few questions?"

"Of course," Suze said. "That's what I'm here for. And, by the way, hi. It's nice to finally meet you."

"It's nice to meet you, too." He flashed a quick smile. Not unfriendly, but somehow too businesslike. "Would you be open to telling me about a past relationship—preferably the first one that springs to mind?" He paused, then added, "Maybe it will help for me to tell you why I'm asking, so it isn't such an open-ended question?"

Suze shrugged flirtatiously. "This is a pretty open-ended experiment anyway...."

Brendan laughed. "I know it. A bit crazy, right? Thank you for bearing with it. Okay, so the reason I'm asking is simply because the way we talk about love says so much about how we see ourselves and what we hope for in life. In some ways we are driven to repeat our relationships. We are attracted to the same qualities. We make the same mistakes. We make choices that are reactions to what we've learned in the past. When you talk about an important relationship, it's a good way for me to absorb all this stuff about you." There was a sparkle in his eye. "Plus, I might learn the way into your heart."

"You just might," Suze said. He radiated confidence, this man. She could see why he was so successful. Her initial hesitance faded. Brendan was definitely her type. Maybe he was onto a good thing with this elaborate blind dating. She was willing to take it seriously, for now at least. "Okay, so, I'm a serial monogamist. I had a high school boyfriend, a college boyfriend, and a postcollege boyfriend. Approximately four years each. I swear that wasn't a deliberate plan, even though I'm sort of a control freak. Each of them was, I have to say, a very good match for me. They were all high achievers, like I am, but thoughtful and loving. I really can't complain.

"My postcollege boyfriend, Craig, is the one I'm going to tell you about because I really thought we'd get married. We met in business school, and we were both very driven. Just completely and obviously well matched. When we started dating, nobody noticed. Literally. Like they'd assumed we were already together. Plus, he was half Korean, which would have made my mother happy. Not that she gets to decide whom I marry. We were both really hard workers who thought the whole work-life balance concept was completely silly. Love what you do and you don't need to worry about balance. For the most part."

"Yes!" Brendan said. "That's what I've always said—kids hate school and adults hate work. That's where we go wrong—making work into a chore. We need to find our passions."

"Right! Except of course there are jobs it would be very hard to love. I mean, personally I would hate being a sanitation worker," Suze said.

"Oh, right. Me, too," said Brendan. "We need to—"

"We need to check our entitlement."

"Exactly."

"Anyway, Craig and I were focused on building our careers, and along the way we went out to dinner and on trips and did all the things that happy couples do together…and we *were* happy."

"But?"

"It was too...easy. Flat. We had settled into life, and I could see us going on like that for years. Adding in kids, buying a house. It was a cookie-cutter life in the making."

"So no cookies for you?" Brendan asked.

"Truthfully? I'm pretty hungry right now," Suze said. "I was too nervous to eat before I came here."

"I'm on it," Brendan said, turning on his phone to send a quick text.

"I didn't mean—"

"No, I'm glad you said something. I'm starving, too."

Suze continued. "Ultimately, the reason I left Craig is that I was bored. He made me boring. I made him boring. Whatever it was, there just wasn't enough..."

"Enough cookies?" Brendan said as a server put down a huge tray of assorted cookies that, impossible though it was, seemed to be freshly baked.

"Exactly," Suze laughed.

"But seriously, you broke up over boredom. Does that mean you've never had your heart broken?"

"To be honest, I'm not wired that way. I guess I'm just practical. You know how people say, 'If it's meant to be, it's meant to be'? That's how I am. I was just born this way."

"So no heartbreak, no big disappointments in life?"

"I aim low," Suze joked.

"I doubt that," Brendan said.

"Okay, it must be that I pick reasonable goals and work hard to accomplish them. I'm the opposite of a drama queen. So you can see why I have to be careful not to get stuck in a boring life."

"What's the antidote?"

"To boredom? You know, I think the antidote is being adventurous. I like to scuba dive, skydive, and ski. It's easier to be brave when you don't stand in your own way."

"I like that!" Brendan said.

"Kind of like being willing to search through any number of women to find the right match…" Suze was trying to steer the conversation to Brendan. Would he reveal anything about himself? Anything about why he was doing this and where she stood?

"It might be bravery. It might be cowardice. But, say what you will, it's certainly not boring."

"Here's to that." Suze lifted her wineglass, and though Brendan's glass seemed to hold water, he clinked it against hers.

"To adventure," he said.

This date, Suze told herself, was going very well. "Now how about you?" she tried. "What about your sordid past?"

"I appreciate you asking—but first I have a few more questions for you." Brendan was so easy to talk to—Suze found herself confessing far more than she usually would on a first date. This man, this house, she could see herself slipping so easily into this life.…

CHAPTER 15

MOMENTS AFTER SUZE accepted a second glass of wine, she saw Brendan glance at his watch. Abruptly, or so it seemed to Suze, he excused himself. Suze found herself mystified. Had she said something wrong? What had started to feel like a regular date, even a good one, apparently wasn't going to pan out that way. Was it over? Brendan had told her to "sit tight." Suze looked around. The books on the shelves were organized by color and height. The desk had nothing on it besides an elegant leather desk set and some sculptural brass paperweights. All of it suddenly seemed like a stage. She still knew nothing at all about Brendan—whether he owned this house or had rented it to create an illusion.…Suze was lost in speculation when another man walked into the library to join her. He appeared to be in his midforties—not quite as handsome as Brendan, but he introduced himself with a certain quiet charm.

"I'm Miguel," he said. "Thank you for enduring this." He swept an arm across the room as if to acknowledge that although the process was strange, it couldn't take place in a nicer venue.

"I'm managing," Suze said with a laugh. This had to be the guy. Older. A little less perfect. Or…not? What a crazy game this was! Suze took a sip of wine. She didn't know much about wine, but one thing she knew for sure. This was more complex and delicious than the Pinots Noirs she picked for their pretty labels at Trader Joe's. Brendan, Miguel, some yet-to-be-presented Bachelor Number Three. What did it matter? Bring on the next! Suze was starting to enjoy herself.

CHAPTER 16

THE MEETING HAD been called for 9:00 p.m., and they had been very clear about not being late, but Janey had a good excuse. She'd interviewed for a job at a well-financed new production company, landed it in the room, and been taken out for a celebratory dinner. (It helped that two of the three executives she met with had been colleagues for years.) Anyway, there was no way she was going to cut short a great moment in her actual life for a mystery man. He would just have to wait. *You know what?* Janey told herself. *If I'm disqualified for having priorities, then I'm not the right woman for the job.*

When Janey got home from the meeting, she tapped on the window of the car that was already waiting outside her bungalow.

"Give me half an hour," she told the driver.

Janey was tired and exhilarated from the meeting. She threw on a gray silk dress, going for pretty but not trying too hard. Hurriedly, she applied makeup, then headed for the door. She closed the door behind her, then realized she'd forgotten lipstick.

Whatever, it doesn't matter, she said to herself. Then she stopped, standing still in front of the door. *No, it does matter.* Not the lipstick. Sure, a guy should be able to love her without sultry red lips. But love. Love mattered. Janey spent ten hours at the office every day. Her commitment was the reason she'd had so much success in her field. But didn't she want a boyfriend, a husband, one day a family, just as much as she wanted to be intellectually fulfilled? And yet she devoted almost no time to that desire.

It does matter, she told herself again. *It's random and crazy, but who knows where love lies?* For all her talk about making a reality show of this strange man's vetting of potential wives, Janey wanted the fairy tale to come true. She hoped against hope that the mystery man would somehow prove to be her prince, and she was willing to make an effort. She unlocked the door and rushed back in to grab a lipstick from the powder room.

By the time they rolled up to the Bel Air mansion, it was 10:05 p.m. Janey rang the doorbell and waited. No response. After a couple of minutes she rang again, and one of the women who had interviewed her, the one with blue glasses, opened the door. She seemed like she'd rushed to the door, but she greeted Janey like an old friend.

"I'm so sorry I'm late," Janey said. "You told me to be on time, and I respect that. But I have a good excuse—I got a new job! Today! Right now!"

"Well, congratulations! You said you wouldn't be jobless for long. Clearly your confidence was justified," the woman, who introduced herself as Alicia, said with a smile.

"Full disclosure, I am also a notoriously bad judge of time. It's

100 percent true that I just got the job and had dinner with them and came straight here, but I want it on the record that I'm always fifteen minutes late. Reliably."

Alicia chuckled. "Good to know," she said. "In the grand scheme of things, what's fifteen minutes?"

"*Thank* you!" Janey said. "Let's put that on a T-shirt and retire."

Alicia led Janey out a set of French doors, through a courtyard, and down to a patio with a tiled infinity pool. "You can't see it now, but there's a view of the ocean straight ahead. On a clear day it looks like the infinity pool flows right into it. Here, have a seat," she said, directing Janey to a small table with votives and a vase of flowers.

"You had me at 'infinity pool,'" Janey said.

Janey was happily drinking a mint tea when she was joined by a man who introduced himself as Rory.

"I know this is a strange way to meet—" he said.

"You think?" Janey said.

Rory had an easy laugh. "I can see you're not shy."

"Nope, sorry. Being shy is a waste of energy, right? I mean, love isn't about being careful to say the right thing. It's just luck of the draw. Chemistry. You like me, I like you—we figure it out or we don't. Sure, I'm nervous. But so what? I could spout a million clichés about love, but ultimately I don't think it should be too hard for you to find your match. If it's hard to pick, then she's not right. Your only hurdle should be whether she likes you back. But in your case, let's be honest, you increased your chances of that when you threw ten million dollars into the pot."

"You think that was a mistake?"

"Honestly? Totally. As soon as you're using money to attract a woman, you've established a dynamic that might never change."

"But here you are! Aren't you a worthwhile candidate?"

"Of course I am. To me the money means I'm dealing with a grown-up. Someone who is serious about finding love."

"But you don't think any other worthwhile candidates might feel the same?"

"Yes, but…wait…" Janey was stuck. "Okay, point for you. I concede that this is a roundabout but viable way to meet women who aren't gold diggers. *If* you have a good filter."

Rory laughed. "Am I a good filter?"

Janey gasped. "You're just a filter? I thought you were the guy!" She punched his arm. "Oh, dude, you had me going there. Who are you, then? Who is *he*? Honestly, I'm kind of glad it isn't you. I like you, but I wasn't feeling it, you know?"

"I'll try not to take that personally," Rory said. They talked for a while longer, Rory asking her about her past relationships and goals in life, but allowing room for the conversation to wander. After some time he stood up and reached out to shake her hand. "It's been great talking to you. But you'll have to excuse me." He left the table and walked back up to the house.

Good Lord, Janey said to herself. She looked around. The garden that stretched out before her was quiet; the pool reflected a sliver of moon. *Was* this evening being taped? She went over to the outdoor kitchen and snooped around, looking for any little red lights or suspicious stuffed animals, but there was no nanny cam to be found. A golden reality-TV opportunity, squandered! She knew exactly where the cameras should be positioned. Ideally they'd have a little more light, of course, but not so much that it ruined the moment. Rory had asked her about heartbreak earlier—this was heartbreak right here, this utter waste of real-life drama and intrigue.

The glass door opened again, and a new man was briefly silhouetted as he stepped out of the house. First a hot new job, now these attractive men emerging one after another. This was turning out to be quite a day. The new guy, Tony, was tall and African American. He gave her a kind of *I have no idea* shrug as he walked toward her.

"Are you a filter, too?" Janey burst out, not bothering to make small talk.

"A filter." Tony looked down at himself, appeared to appraise his arms. "Not totally sure what you mean. But I do wear contact lenses, if that's what you're getting at." He smiled, and Janey took note. This man had a heart-stoppingly good smile.

Janey poured more hot water into her tea. "Are you Mr. Man of Mystery? Please enlighten me. I don't know how much longer I can take the suspense."

"Ah, no. I'm just here to get to know you a bit better."

"A filter! I knew it."

"That wasn't in the job description, but if that's how you'd like to see it, sure."

"Okay, just so we're clear. Now you can…do your thing." Janey gave an overly dramatic flourish, gesturing for him to get started, and he complied. This Tony was very easy on the eyes. Whatever their conversation was meant to achieve, she was perfectly content to draw it out for as long as possible.

"Let me ask you a question," he said. "What do you think is the secret to a long marriage?"

"It's funny that you ask that," Janey said. "When I was doing my thesis in film school, I interviewed a bunch of couples who had been together for at least forty years."

"What made you decide to do that?"

"I did it because my parents were in the middle of a divorce—after twenty-five years together. They had made it so far, only to give up. I wanted to know what it takes to get past the big hurdles, past raising your children, past unexpected life changes, past distractions or affairs. What sustains a relationship into 'till death do us part'?"

"And what did you find?" Tony said.

"Well, I was only in grad school, remember, so I can't say my insights were exceptionally original. But a few things stood out: neither person can be a perfectionist; it really helps if you make each other laugh; and the more fortunate you are in terms of steady income and health, the better your prospects. But, above all, there was just one simple thing. Both people had to believe in the commitment of marriage. They had to have faith in what they had, and to recognize that they probably wouldn't be better off in any other relationship. At some point, when things sucked—because in every relationship they sometimes do—each couple decided to look at the big picture, to believe that they could turn a corner and fall in love all over again."

"And you, do you believe in the commitment of marriage?"

"I do," Janey said, as if it were a solemn vow. They both laughed. "Do you?" she said.

"I do," he said. They laughed again.

"You're sure you're not the man of mystery? Because this is kind of nice."

"I'm afraid not, but I agree. This is kind of nice."

There was something about this guy. She instinctively liked him. She continued, "Whatever 'the commitment of marriage' means. What I believe is that whole idea of making it work. People can grow apart, and people can surprise you, but I think if you're honest from the start and know each other as well as two people can, then you have a fighting chance. It's not all about putting the toilet seat down."

"Phew," Tony said.

"Speaking of being open and honest from the start, do you think you might tell me what the hell this is all about?"

Tony laughed, a big, friendly laugh. He seemed so real and genuine, and yet he was part of this whole mysterious process. "Honestly?" he said. "I have no fucking clue. All I know is that I'm supposed to talk to you, get a feel for who you are, and some dude might or might not pick you to win millions of dollars."

"Well, what do you think? Am I worth it?"

Tony shook his head, laughing. "In my book you are. I'm totally rooting for you. If you want to end up with a billionaire nutcase."

"He's a nutcase?"

"Like I said, I have no fucking clue! Never met the guy."

"If I marry him, do you think you and I could have a side thing?" Janey said. Then, "I am totally kidding, of course. That joke probably ruined my shot. Classic self-sabotage. But some guys like that, right? Please report that I was *kidding*. Do you have a notepad? Could you write it down?"

"I've got it right here," Tony said, tapping his forehead. And there was that killer smile again. Swoon.

CHAPTER 17

WHEN CAROLINE EMERGED from her interview, it felt like she was exiting an amusement park ride. She'd been transported to another world, one that felt thrilling and stomach-dropping at the same time. She would process it when she got home, since Alicia had told her that a driver would be arriving momentarily. Stepping out onto the front porch, Caroline was shocked to see two other women waiting. Everyone had been so attentive to her that she'd actually started to feel like she was the only remaining candidate.

"Well, hello, ladies," said one of the women. She had pretty brown hair and a wide smile. "I'm Janey," she said. "Oh, my God, can you believe this?"

Caroline introduced herself, as did another woman, named Suze. Suze was drop-dead gorgeous. She might have been part Asian; she was immaculately groomed and her sheath dress looked like it had been designed with her in mind.

"What the hell just happened in there?" Caroline said.

"All I know is we got swag bags!" Janey said, holding up a

heavy-stock gift bag. "I've never gotten a swag bag from a date before."

"Does this count as being paid for a date?" Suze asked, rooting through her bag. She paused, holding up a box. "I'm guessing the watch alone is worth thousands of dollars."

"I think the whole experience falls into the category of being paid for a date—" Caroline said.

"Except we only get the big bucks if we win!" Janey laughed.

"Look at these!" Caroline said, opening a little cloth pouch and pulling out a pair of diamond studs. "Did we all get the same?"

Suze and Janey dug into their bags. Suze's earrings were a different style—daggerlike, with four smaller diamonds set in a row. And Janey, who didn't have pierced ears, found a diamond pavé bracelet.

"Holy shit," Janey said.

"Thousands of dollars, you say? eBay here I come!" Caroline grinned.

Janey looked back at the house. "Are we the only ones? Are we three the finalists?"

"So it would seem," said Suze. "If I were running a ten-million-dollar wife contest, I would definitely narrow it down to three."

There was a moment of silence, then they all burst into laughter.

"Let me get this straight. Would you place the billboard on Sunset for maximum impact?" Janey asked in her best reporter's tone.

"Would you invite said candidates to your Bel Air estate, then send handsome men to flirt with them until midnight?" Caroline chimed in.

"Would you—"

"Oh, my God, is it midnight?" Suze exclaimed. "Shit, shit, shit…" She pulled out her phone and hurriedly typed into it.

"FingerLock match required," her phone said. Suze touched a button with her thumb.

"FingerLock match achieved," the phone said, and Suze heaved a sigh of relief.

"What the hell is going on with you, James Bond?" Janey asked.

"Is your phone about to turn into a pumpkin?" Caroline teased.

Suze blushed. "I was unable to investigate the owner of this house. It's owned by a corporation with no other trackable assets. So I set up a remote alert in case I found myself in danger."

Janey whistled. "Nice!"

"You are way out of my league," Caroline added. "I'm so impressed. Now tell me this. Can your FingerLock technology keep my mother from reading my e-mails?"

"Most definitely," Suze said. "It's set for release in the spring, but I can add you to the beta list."

"Would you? I'll put in a good word for you with our future husband, whoever he is."

A black Town Car pulled up to the house. The driver stepped out. "Ms. Ellis?" he said.

"That's me," Janey said. She stepped forward, then turned to the other two women. "Can't we carpool? I, for one, am not done with you guys. Maybe we can get to the bottom of this."

"Count me in," said Caroline.

"Yes, in theory, but shouldn't we at least confirm that we all live in the same direction?" Suze asked.

"You should win," Janey said. Then, to Caroline: "She should totally win."

CHAPTER 18

"**I'M DRAGGING YOU** out of your way. It really doesn't make any sense for either of you to come all the way to mid-Wilshire," Suze said.

"Don't even worry about it," Janey said, stretching back in the plush leather seat. "We need you. What's a gratuitous tour of Los Angeles when ten million dollars are at stake?"

"Especially if this car has beverages," Caroline said. She tapped the driver's shoulder. "Excuse me, but do you have any beverages?"

The driver wordlessly handed back three bottles of water, one at a time.

"Oh," said Caroline. "It is a beverage, I concede. Not exactly the beverage I had in mind, but a beverage nonetheless."

There was no traffic, and they flew east on the 10. Caroline snuck a look to her left, assessing the women next to her. If this was a beauty contest, she was definitely going to lose. Janey was long limbed and had an effortless, beachy beauty. There was nothing particularly exotic about her, but her features were perfectly even and appealing. Plus, she was very witty and confident. Caroline already wanted to be friends with her. Suze was even more impressive. She was clearly a tech genius, a nerd trapped in a bikini body. To Caroline, Suze seemed like a dream wife, as if someone had handed all the men of the world a wish list, and Suze was the universal ideal. If Suze was Prince Charming's type, then Caroline knew she was out of the running.

"Check it out!" Janey exclaimed, pointing. They were driving toward a brightly lit billboard that said, LOVE IS HARD TO FIND BUT EASY TO RECOGNIZE. ARE YOU THE ONE? TENMILLION-DOLLARPROPOSAL.COM.

"Not to split hairs, but if we're truly the final round, that billboard should have come down already," Suze said.

"Maybe we're not," Caroline said. "Maybe we're just tonight's candidates. Or maybe we're the LA contingent. Frankly, if this goes on much longer, I might bail."

Janey held up a hand. "Wait, before we get to when and why we'll quit, let's pool our knowledge. Do we know anything about this guy? Who is he? What's he looking for?"

The driver cleared his throat. "Is anyone getting out?"

"Oh! Here we are," Suze said. They had no idea how long the car had been stopped. They were in front of a sleek, modern apartment building.

"I don't want to be rude, but I'd love to talk with you guys more. Should we go get a coffee?" Janey said.

"Let's," Suze said. "This guy knows everything about us, and we know nothing about him. Let's even the score."

"Can we do it tomorrow?" Caroline asked. "It's already way past my bedtime."

They made a plan to meet, then Janey turned to the driver. "Don't tell him we're conspiring, okay?"

"What if I'm your man?" the driver said. Three heads whipped around to check him out. He was middle aged, with a rakish grin.

"Oh, my God, are you serious right now?" Janey asked.

The driver laughed. "I was just kidding," he said. But *was* he?

CHAPTER 19

ENTERING THE APARTMENT, Suze realized she was still hungry for something other than chocolate chip cookies. She made herself one of her killer grilled cheese sandwiches. She usually read a magazine when she was eating alone, but tonight she just stared out the window. Her view wasn't much during the day, but at night she could see the lights of the city all the way to downtown. She was calm on the outside, but internally still wired with curiosity. She sat down at the counter and unpacked the gift bag, taking more time now to study the items she'd only rifled through. There were some bath products, elegantly packaged; a candle from the French perfumer Diptyque; a white cashmere scarf. She held the soft scarf to her cheek. Its whiteness seemed to embody the promise of this generous mystery man—a clean, perfect world of luxury might be handed to her just for being…the right one, whatever that might be. Lastly she took out the earrings. She removed the pearl studs that she had worn every day for six years and put the diamond daggers in. Sharp and brilliant, they seemed to transform her.

Before putting the pearl studs away in her jewelry box, she

rolled them in her palm. Wow, she had been wearing these earrings for a long time. Craig had given them to her on their first anniversary. That night they were in New York City for Christmas, and he took her to the fanciest restaurant she'd ever been to. At the end of dinner he pulled out the small black box. She was instantly terrified—she wasn't ready to get engaged, she was still in business school! But he quickly said, "Don't worry—it's not a ring." She had been so delighted with the gift because, to her memory, it was the first gift she'd ever received that was completely out of the blue. Craig had just wanted her to know how much he loved her, beyond what he could ever say, and that night she could see it in his eyes.

Now she looked at the pearls, pale against the velvet of the jewelry box. When had they begun to look so tired? They still radiated a warmth and the sense of home that she treasured. She opened her computer and went to Craig's Facebook page. She didn't want him back. She didn't want anything from him. But what was wrong with missing someone who had been the most important person in her life for so long? Should she never see or speak to him again just because she'd been too young and dumb not to marry him?

Craig hadn't updated his page for three months, but his last post told her everything she wanted to know. It was a picture of him, hairline a little compromised, but as happy as she'd ever seen him. He was standing next to an attractive woman who was tagged in the photo. Natalia. The two of them beamed, radiant, and the caption said, *I asked and she answered…yes!* Craig was engaged.

Suze could see in their photos that the affection that had once been hers alone now belonged to Natalia. She wouldn't reach out to Craig, not now and not ever.

Suze closed her laptop and went to rinse her face, washing the tears away as soon as they appeared. The truth, which she would have told Brendan earlier this evening if she'd thought it through, was that her heart had indeed been broken before. It was just that she'd been the one to do it.

CHAPTER 20

THE NEXT DAY they converged at a low-key bar in Hollywood for an after-work drink.

Janey was late. Suze and Caroline, waiting for her to arrive, fell into talk about their respective jobs.

Caroline said, "The gratitude I get for just showing up—you can see that these kids have never had anyone rooting for them. No adults who introduced them to the world and their place in it. Think what life would look like from that perspective. They just kind of floated out into this scary, unsafe environment and did whatever they could to survive. But they are hungry for direction. They are dying to learn any other way of life, especially one in which they aren't fighting for their lives."

"That is really heavy," Suze said. "I spend all day meeting with innovators, and none of them are solving the real problems of the world. I mean, today I tried a prototype for temperature-sensitive clothing that heats or cools your body to your desired temperature."

"Really? That's so cool!" Caroline said.

"Cool, sure, but these are MIT engineers, supersmart, and

they're campaigning for VC money that could go anywhere in the world."

"You can't think of it that way," Janey said, sliding into the booth and the conversation. "Rich people invest to get richer, and they give to charity to help the world. That's how it works. If they invest in the charities, it all goes haywire. Trust me."

"I think there's another way...." Suze said.

"The divide is so big—I don't know if there's any way to bridge the gap between the haves and the have-nots," Caroline said. "Unless I win this marriage proposal. In that case, there will be a very long bridge connecting me and Prince Charming."

"For ten million dollars you can build a pretty long bridge," Janey said.

"I wouldn't recommend it," Suze said.

"I haven't really stopped to think about the money," Caroline said. "Who has ten million dollars just sitting around? It must be the tip of the iceberg."

"Well, assuming he marries the woman, it comes right back to him anyway, right?" Suze said.

"I would like to take a vacation somewhere," Janey said dreamily. "Hawaii. I've never been there. Or maybe the Galápagos. People like that travel to exotic places all the time, because their houses are so luxurious that it takes more than a nice hotel and a beach to motivate them to leave."

"I wouldn't mind vacationing in that house we went to. A weekend there would be the nicest vacation I've ever had," said Caroline.

"Vacations sound nice, but also think of what it would do for our careers!" Suze said. "I could make my own investments instead of making recommendations to my bosses."

"I could rebuild the learning center," Caroline said. "I would definitely do that."

"I would love to never think about money again. I wouldn't have to keep track of whether there was enough money in my account to pay my bills or to go to a certain restaurant. I would be completely free of that. Maybe forever," Janey said.

"I'm worried that we're jinxing ourselves by just having this conversation," Caroline said.

"We don't even know what the reality is," Janey said. "But we're all smart women. Let's figure this out. What do we know about this guy? Why is he doing this? There has to be a hitch. Does he even have the money?"

"Now, that's a good question. Maybe it's all a scam," said Suze.

"Is he hot? Is he a sexist pig looking for a high-end mail-order bride?" Caroline asked.

Suze pulled out her phone. "I did do some research. The house we just visited is registered to a privately owned corporation called Estes Realty, but I couldn't find any other information about it. It was just incorporated last year, right before purchasing the house for a little under six million dollars. As far as I can tell, it was new construction and it was purchased *before* being listed on the market."

"Wow, you're good," Janey said.

"I guess mansions cost that much," Caroline said with awe. "I never thought about it."

Suze continued, "So that speaks to someone with considerable resources and connections. Unless he's renting. Or being financed."

"I did some sleuthing, too," Janey said. "In my old job—which, by the way, sucked—the Marketing Department bought space from the billboard company he used for those ads. So I had my friend Joey, in Marketing, give them a call to find out who leased the space for the ten-million-dollar billboard. Joey couldn't get *anything* out of his contact there. And Joey is, like, the most skilled gossip in all of West Hollywood. He thinks there must have been a nondisclosure with penalties attached. Apparently, that's the only thing that can keep people in Hollywood quiet. So again, our man's definitely got some power and connections. And a good lawyer."

"That's what makes me nervous," Caroline said. "How come there's so much secrecy? It can't say anything good about a person that he has to be so private."

"Well, he's rich. And he's publicizing that he's rich and single. I can see why he wouldn't want to release his name before he's made his choice," Suze reasoned.

"But say you're picked," Caroline said. "Then what? Does the elaborate hunt end all at once?"

"Or will we have further challenges, with ongoing incentives?" Suze speculated.

"Scavenger hunts," Caroline said.

"Slaying of Medusa," Janey joked. "In all seriousness, if we're attracted to the mystery, we're gonna be let down. There's a man behind the curtain, and he's no wizard. Once he picks someone, I bet dating the dude is the same old crapshoot."

"But at least we'd have a lot to talk about on the first date," Caroline said.

"I have to admit I like the process," Suze said. "I appreciate his analytic approach. And his house is exactly to my taste. I know that's superficial. I'm not saying I'd marry the guy, but he's already got a few points in his favor."

"You liked that house, seriously?" Janey asked. "It's fine, I guess. But I can tell a designer did it for him. There were, like, 'vignettes' on every flat surface. A vase, a sculpture, a stack of books. Totally contrived."

"I like that it's a house. And that my mother doesn't live there," Caroline joked.

"Hey, did you have cute guys interviewing you last night? I was seriously hoping one of mine was *him*," Janey said. "But I know they weren't."

"You know? How?" asked Suze.

"I have my ways of getting information," Janey said. "I had Rory and Tony. They were both superhot. Good candidates for my soon-to-be-launched reality-TV contest. I'm thinking I'll call it *The Ten-Million-Dollar Marriage Proposal*."

"So original," Caroline said.

"I had Brendan and Miguel," Suze said. "It's strange. The minute Miguel walked in, I was sure he was the bachelor."

"Why?" Janey asked.

"Frankly, it was because he wasn't as model-perfect as everyone else involved in this project seems to be. But he was so easy to talk to. We somehow ended up discovering that we have a lot in common."

"Like what?" Janey asked.

"Well, we both fantasize about going on long-distance bike rides with our children one day."

"That's really random," Caroline said. "And I'm kind of impressed. I didn't peg you as outdoorsy."

"Oh, I'm not. That was the best part. We both want to bike all day and stay in five-star hotels at night. We're thinking France."

"It sounds like you had an actual date! Forget the ten million. Run away with Miguel!" Caroline said.

Suze laughed. "We may or may not have discussed that."

"Whoa. Miguel is so fired," Janey said.

"Unless he's the millionaire, which is entirely possible," said Caroline. She had met with only one person, a pleasant-looking guy named Nicholas who had been particularly interested in her work trying to change the school-to-prison pipeline. So often people glazed over when she talked about what she did. Almost everyone in LA was in "the industry" and preferred to talk about TV shows, movies, and celebrity scandals. Caroline had cancelled her cable three years ago when she found herself spending far too much time watching junk, and she hadn't looked back.

For once Caroline hadn't tried too hard to be a perfect date, to be whatever he might want her to be. There was something about this process that made her feel like she might as well risk being herself, for better or worse. There was nothing to lose.

Now she was glad to keep the conversation focused on the men who had interviewed Janey and Suze. Ridiculous as it was, she wanted to keep her encounter private. She found that as soon as she talked about an experience, she became more removed from it. Overanalysis took the spontaneous and imperfect moments in life and categorized them.

In the past, as soon as she put them in the hands of her girl-friends, her dates had been reduced to a critique of his clothes, his manners, the awkwardness with which he'd said good-bye. After that kind of judgment, how could you possibly be excited at the prospect of a second date? Caroline felt the same way about this process. Judging it too much might ruin it. So she asked the girls questions about themselves and their experiences, all the while wondering, *but not deciding,* what her own night meant and what might come of it.

CHAPTER 21

JANEY HAD A pile of scripts to read that night, and each of them proved to be some variation on the fish-out-of-water theme: a misfit with supernatural powers; a big-city lawyer moves to the country to follow her dream of becoming a farmer; a former beauty queen takes a job as a bounty hunter; and so on. It was well past midnight when she finally threw the last script to the floor and turned out the light.

Exhausted though she was, Janey couldn't sleep. She swept her arm across the empty bed next to her, wishing she had company. But this man of mystery, if he ever revealed himself—would he deign to sleep in her bed? Could a man who lived in a house like that ever be comfortable in her Craftsman bungalow, with its low-slung ceilings, rough floors, and single bathroom? With bad water pressure?

All she could do was have faith in the process. If he were a playboy, making a game out of picking a wife—then he would never have picked Janey. Or Suze or Caroline, for that matter. They were all, in their own ways, down-to-earth. Surely a man who chose them could slum it here in her pad. He would have to, she told herself. She wasn't going to mold herself into his world.

She could see herself having that conversation with him, the one where he'd chosen her, and she was reminding him that she had a career to think of, and he would have to respect that.

"Of course," he would say, taking her hand in his. They would be out on his patio, appreciating the sweeping views over a bottle of wine. *"I've been wanting to downsize to someplace more cozy."*

Janey would hold up her hand to stop him. *"Let's not jump the gun here,"* she'd say. *"We have plenty of time for all of that."*

"Only the rest of our lives," he'd say, and lean in to kiss her.

Janey rolled over, knocking two pillows off the bed. She looked at the clock. It was 1:30 and she still hadn't slept. She had to get up in five and a half hours! She couldn't function on that little sleep. She reached over and reset her alarm to 9:00 a.m. In her new job, thankfully, she set her own hours.

She pulled her laptop out from under the bed and opened it up. The studies said that looking at a screen in the middle of the night was the worst thing for insomnia, but she didn't care. If this bachelor was going to keep her up all night, she would at least use the time productively. She addressed an e-mail to herself and gave it a subject line: *Story Ideas.*

CHAPTER 22

THE YARD BEHIND Caroline's mother's house was brown in the porch light. As the person who'd insisted her mother turn off the sprinklers and apply for a water-saving rebate from the city, Caroline couldn't complain, but it was still depressing.

With a furtive look over her shoulder to make sure her mother and sister were asleep, Caroline lit a cigarette. It was an old bad habit, and really her mother couldn't fault her for it, since her own insistence that Caroline be skinny had driven her to cigarettes as a teenager. Now she indulged only once a month, max, and only in moments of stress.

Caroline exhaled. It was ridiculous that she was stressed out about this crazy love contest when she had so many other things to worry about. *Admit it,* she told herself, *you're looking for an easy fix.* She didn't want or expect a gallant stranger to sweep her off her feet, solve her housing and other financial woes, and leave her to pursue a life of charitable work. In fact, that was the opposite of what she wanted. If love was entwined with salvation, could it be trusted?

For the umpteenth time Caroline resolved to pull herself out of the running.

But what if she actually liked him? What if they liked each other? What if they were soul mates?

As weird and unlikely as this whole rigmarole was, Caroline couldn't help but harbor a small, irrational hope that everything would work out. He would pick her, and he would pick her because he saw her for who she really was, and they would live happily ever after. It was unlikely, but it wasn't impossible. No matter what else had gone on and would go on surrounding their meeting, they were still just two people who hadn't met each other, and in that simple equation there was a whole world of possibility.

What if she never heard from him again? How long would he leave her in this maddening state of limbo?

CHAPTER 23

SUZE WAS GOOGLING Mr. Moneybags. She knew it was a useless exercise—she had already googled him, the contest, the corporation that had purchased his house, to death. She'd even checked to see who had registered the domain of the website that was hosting the contest. Her fantasy was to find him on social media or, failing that, perhaps to stumble on a sibling who'd blabbed about the contest. But it was not meant to be. He had total control of the flow of information, and she would simply have to wait. Suze shut down her computer and crawled into bed. It was beyond frustrating to have such big stakes, and no idea of when or how they would play out.

Lying in bed, she stared at the ceiling. And then it dawned on her. She couldn't track down any of Mr. Moneybags' personal information, but the way the contest was being conducted told her plenty. Suze realized, with great certainty, that Mr. Moneybags would contact all three finalists tomorrow. This contest was not slow and drawn out. He was not reveling in the suspense. He wanted to find someone, and he'd used his financial position to attempt to do so as efficiently as possible. Tomorrow her life might change. And yet even tomorrow was too long to wait.

After half an hour of restlessness Suze went to the bathroom and popped half an Ambien. Whatever the news might be tomorrow, she wanted to be ready for it.

CHAPTER 24

THE NEXT MORNING, when Suze arrived at her desk, there was an envelope waiting for her. Her first name, written in careful calligraphy, was the only thing on the envelope. It had obviously been delivered by messenger, and she had no doubt at first glance that this was it. She was about to find out if she'd won or lost this lottery of love.

After hiding the unopened envelope carefully in her desk drawer, she went to the café and ordered the usual: a regular mochaccino. She brought it back to her office and sat still for a moment, warming her hands on the cup.

She was pretty sure that this meant she hadn't won. There had been many envelopes in Suze's past, and for the most part they had heralded success. She had known without looking that she'd gotten into every college to which she'd applied. The same was true for business school. But the handful of times she hadn't been accepted to a program or landed a fellowship or been offered a job, she had felt doubt. This was a virtue. She never doubted herself, but she could always sense when the match wasn't perfect. Then again, this contest was unlike any she'd ever entered. There were too many variables. Who could say what a perfect match with the presumably unmet mystery man might feel like? Certainly, neither Janey nor Caroline had more reason to feel confident than she did.

Suze took out the envelope. Would she be disappointed if she lost? Did she even want to win? She was 100 percent certain that even if this slim envelope held a check for ten million dollars, she hadn't found her perfect match. Maybe *he* had, but she hadn't. Not only was the process deeply flawed but the odds were simply against it. And yet…ten million dollars was life-changing. She would carefully consider any proposal that came with that bonus.

She tore open the envelope. The letter inside was neither long nor formulaic.

Dear Suze,

First, my lawyers tell me I have to write this: This letter falls under the confidentiality agreement you signed when you filled out the application. Any violation will cause injury that would be difficult to quantify, but would cause me irreparable damage. Please have another look at your copy of the agreement if you have questions about that.

Okay, now that that's out of the way, I want to say how fortunate I feel to have had the chance to "meet" you through my counselors. Every step of the way, I was impressed not just by your accomplishments, your analytical mind, your self-

awareness, but by your ability to balance these qualities with warmth and a sense of fun. I have great admiration for you, but, to be frank (why belabor this, right? You've been too generous with your time already), I don't think we're a match. I'm sorry if this is disappointing to you, but somehow I doubt it will be. You're probably a step ahead of me in knowing what would be best here.

Suze, you are an amazing woman. I wish you every happiness, and I know you will find love easily. You deserve him, and he deserves you. And who knows, maybe I'll find myself a guest at your wedding in the not-too-distant future.

Yours,
Miguel

So that was that. Suze folded the letter and put it back into the envelope. She had been right after all. Miguel was Mr. Moneybags. He was the one she had liked best, and she had gambled on that, treating him like her date instead of an interviewer. Now she was left with the same questions she might have any time a guy didn't call her for a second date. What had gone wrong? What had been missing? The letter offered no clues. Suddenly she realized something: this was the first time a guy hadn't called her for a second date.

She hated to lose, damnit. Suze took a sip of her coffee and let the feeling settle. She had wanted to get to know Miguel more than she cared to admit. It was over, no matter what she wanted.

In a moment she found a small smile creeping across her face. He was so sure that she would find happiness, he almost had her convinced. Besides, it had been fun.

Suze picked up her phone, thinking she'd text Janey and Caroline to see what they'd heard, but then thought better of it. Let them find out in their own time. She was out of this game.

CHAPTER 25

ISABELLE HADN'T BEEN this excited since Caroline was a semifinalist in the Miss Teen Santa Monica Off-Season Fruit Pageant, a questionable concept and perhaps, therefore, the scene of Caroline's all-time biggest pageant success.

When Caroline came downstairs, breakfast was already on the table, a goat cheese and asparagus scramble (her favorite) and glazed doughnuts from the Mister Donut down the street—a much-fantasized-about but extremely rare indulgence. Isabelle's daughters never had processed sugar if she had anything to do with it. Isabelle whistled cheerily as she set a pitcher of fresh-squeezed orange juice on the table. Yes, Isabelle was very happy.

There was a knock at the door, and Caroline went to answer it. A messenger handed her an envelope. "From Mr. Nicholas," he said, and went back to his car.

Nicholas, Caroline processed. That was the name of her interviewer. But he was too humble to be a millionaire, wasn't he? And probably too young. Neither Suze nor Janey had mentioned meeting a Nicholas. Was she the only one he'd taken the time to interview? Was that man, that Nicholas, her knight in shining armor? Or were the interviewers handling the communications?

"Is that the electrician?" Isabelle screeched from the kitchen. "Tell him it's the outdoor light near the garage. It's been blinking ever since he quote-unquote fixed it, and I'm not paying him again."

"Mom," Caroline tried to stop her. "It's not—"

"You hear me, Caroline?" Isabelle's volume made Caroline wince.

"Got it, Mom," Caroline called back. She quickly hid the envelope in her robe and went into the bathroom, then sat down on the toilet lid to open the letter.

Dear Caroline,

What is the right thing to say here? I loved meeting you. Thank you for the time you spent on my "odd little experiment," as you put it. I especially respect your concern about being with someone who is more settled in life than you are, although I think there are many different ways in which a person can be settled. To help people the way you do in your work shows a deep generosity; it shows how much you have thought about the meaning of life and how we can best spend our time.

To be honest, I felt like the two of us had a chance. But in the clear light of day, I'm hesitant. I'm still not sure what I want. I realize how outrageous that must sound, given what I've put you through. I tend to make my mistakes on a grand scale. And it's probably a mistake to let you go. But I don't want to waste more of your time if I'm simply not ready. So I must take my leave now, hoping we can keep the door open and that at some point in the future you might not refuse my call.

Yours,
Nicholas

Reading the letter, Caroline could hear the soft, calm voice of the man she'd met the other night. So he *was* the millionaire! And he had liked her! She couldn't quite tell from the letter, but it seemed like she had, against all odds, won. She'd landed the lead part. And now they were cancelling the show. He was giving up. Without even trying. Caroline bit her bottom lip, willing herself not to cry. Of course she hadn't won anything. She'd never really dared to dream that she would. But now, to hear how close she'd come…and what had she lost? At the very least, a man who could rescue her from this house, her mother, her debt. And if she dared to dream—Prince Charming, a man whom she might love, a man who chose her from the crowd, a man who could help her make real changes in the world. A soul mate.

This whole time she'd told herself she didn't believe in the contest, or care about it. But the mere possibility it presented had forced her to confront the reality of her life. She was twenty-six years old, living with her mother. Her job, which she loved, would never support her. She hadn't been on a date—hadn't even met someone who interested her—in the ten months since Steven dumped her.

Somehow she had managed to spend three years thinking she had a healthy and loving relationship with a man who felt perfectly comfortable breaking up with her simply by never returning her calls. No arguments, no ultimatums, no *We have to talk,* just utter silence. It had been insulting and devastating. How could she trust someone after that? How could she trust herself? For the brief period of this contest Caroline had allowed herself to hope, to believe that someone might pick her out of a crowd and love her exactly as she was. But even the man who'd invented the contest was wise enough not to be so hopelessly romantic in the end. She was the fool who'd been willing to believe in someone else's misguided fantasy.

Nicholas was right, of course. This was a stupid way to find love. Or to make money, for that matter. But it sure would have been nice. And after daring to hope that her life could actually fall into place, fairy-tale style, she now had to face how far from the truth that was.

Brooke knocked on the door. "Everything okay in there? I have to get ready for school."

"Oh, sure, sorry. Be right out." Caroline threw water on her face and brushed past Brooke before her sister could notice anything. In the kitchen she shoved a doughnut into her mouth and muttered something about her allergies acting up, just in case her mother noticed any redness around her eyes.

"Enjoy!" her mother crowed. "We're celebrating today, aren't we? You're putting yourself out there, Caroline. The only way to make things change is to change them yourself, and you're doing it. I'm so proud of you."

"Thanks, Mom," Caroline said. She didn't want to deceive her mother, but it seemed a shame to let her down so soon.

CHAPTER 26

WHEN ELODY PUT the yellow envelope on Janey's desk, Janey assumed it had been misdelivered. Other than Elody, who hadn't hesitated to follow Janey to her new company, she hadn't told anyone about the job. Even her parents didn't know yet. Nobody knew where she was. But the messenger had found her here. Her eyes jumped down to the signature so that she could identify the sender. Tony. Did she know a Tony? She began to read.

Dear Janey,

It's me. Your filter.

Oh. That Tony. Janey looked up and saw that Elody was still in the doorway, waiting expectantly.

"Is it from him? The mystery man?" Elody asked. Her radar was a little too good sometimes. Janey's eyes jumped down to the bottom of the letter. Her eyes caught the phrase *he does not think you two are a match.* She was being rejected.

"It's him, and he's rejecting me," she told Elody. Janey skimmed the letter, in which Tony thanked her for the time and energy she'd given to "this unorthodox search" and complimented her.

The end said,

I also want to remind you to please respect his privacy and the nondisclosure that you signed. If he does choose anyone, there will be no announcement of a winner, in the hope that the two of them can continue to lead a private life.

Again, it was a delight to meet you. I hope I have the chance again.

Your filter,
Tony

"I'm sorry," Elody said. "You came so close. I'm sure you're disappointed."

"A little, but at least I got a good reality show idea out of it." Janey put the letter down on her still-clean desk. The night before, when she couldn't sleep, she had made a list of show ideas—writers she wanted to approach, areas that might appeal to them. On that list, somewhere in the middle, was the ten-million-dollar marriage proposal idea.

"I must admit I kind of got my hopes up," Elody said. "The type of guy who would go big, risk it all—I could see him falling for you. Things always work out for you. Look how this job fell into your lap."

"I'm bummed," Janey admitted. "It's not that I wanted it to work out for me—I mean, it would have been nice. But as a producer, I wanted the fairy-tale ending most of all. All those women who responded to the billboard were so hopeful that this would be the beginning of the rest of their life. The interviewers were so invested. They seemed to really want it to work out for this guy. The mystery man himself was willing to invest so much to search for his one true love. I really want one woman to emerge from all that effort and expense. Out of all those women, there had to be a Cinderella ready for her Prince Charming. I want it to work out. I want a happy ending!"

"You never stop being a producer, do you?" Elody said teasingly.

"I'm afraid not," Janey chirped, but when Elody turned away, Janey felt a lump in her throat. Being a producer got her only so far. Elody was wrong. Things didn't always work out for her. At work, maybe, but not with men. Sebastian, that cheating bastard. In hindsight, all the signs had been there, and she'd felt like such an idiot when she stumbled across the texts to other women on his cell phone.

Janey walked out onto the lot. Little golf carts drove around, and over by the soundstages workers were unloading an enormous fake snowman, dragging it between tall palm trees. She headed toward the New York street, the outdoor set that was used whenever something took place in New York. Most of the buildings were facades that could be dressed to be a hardware shop today, a deli tomorrow. Janey sat down on the stoop of one of the buildings, looking over subway stairs that led down to a flat wall. This was the place where stories were born and made out of nothing. This street was full of promise—the blank slate for everything she'd worked so hard to achieve. She'd better get to it.

She walked back toward her office, passing the huge murals of classic movies that were painted on the vast, windowless walls of the sets. Across from the door to Janey's office were Humphrey Bogart and Ingrid Bergman, cheek to cheek, three stories tall, with *Casablanca* painted in cursive below them. Janey slipped inside, embarrassed that she cared. It was ridiculous to be disappointed by a man she'd never met. But she did care. How could she be such a go-getter in her career and such a failure in her love life?

Back at her desk, Janey picked up the envelope and studied the label. It had a processing stamp, presumably from the messenger service. "Elody?" she called out. Elody popped back into the office as if she'd been waiting just outside the door. Janey handed her the envelope. "Let's track this. I'm not quite ready to give up."

CHAPTER 27

SUZE ASSUMED THE letter she'd received was the end of it. She and Meredith went out for a postgame happy hour.

"Miguel was so down-to-earth—not at all what you would expect from a millionaire. He was a good conversationalist, a good listener. I've never told anyone so much about myself on the first date. And the crazy part is that I was so interested in him that I forgot to care about the contest. I just wanted to get to know him better. So when he turned out to be the guy, I felt even worse."

"We don't know anything, though, do we? Maybe Miguel was the guy, maybe that letter is another misleading detail, to protect the real millionaire. Maybe there's no money at all. Maybe the whole thing was a scam."

"I wasn't scammed—I'm sure of it. I absolutely didn't release any private information."

"Okay, then a fake. For God-knows-what reason. Maybe he gets off on jerking women around like this."

"Could be," Suze said. "But did you see my earrings?" She was wearing the diamond daggers now, and she'd gotten used to the sparkle. It was time she left Craig behind. "If it's a scam, it's a pretty elaborate, expensive one. I just didn't win. It happens. It wasn't a complete waste of time. I needed to…I needed to let go a little, you know?"

Meredith raised her wineglass to Suze's. "Let's toast to that," she said. "I'm glad you said it, not me."

The next morning Suze was in a meeting, listening to two men pitch their nonprofit: the California Schoolroom. It was an idea she liked—an online clearinghouse where charter schools could pool and redistribute resources—but she knew the executives at Redfield Partners would never go for it. Every time Suze had tried to get them to invest in educational ventures, they'd said no. Still, she was interested enough to hear the pitch.

In the middle of the meeting Meredith came rushing up to the door of her office, then stopped short when she realized that the visitors' chairs were occupied. Meredith retreated, but not before Suze noticed what she was holding: another yellow mailing envelope. For the rest of the pitch Suze tried to push aside fantasies of what that envelope might hold. Sure, that generic envelope could be anything from anyone, but from Meredith's expression Suze guessed—no, she *knew*—that it was from the contest. But she'd already been rejected. What was left to say? Impatient, Suze broke the news to the California Schoolroom guys as gently as she could.

"I'm not saying you don't have a viable product here," she said. "Personally, I love the idea. But I'll never be able to sell the partners on it. They want to wait until we hit our fund-raising target for this year before taking on any nonprofits." Suze ushered them out of the office, then headed straight to Meredith's cubicle.

"Where is it? What is it?" she asked.

"Open it!" Meredith flung the envelope into Suze's hands.

Somehow, by the time they crossed the hall to Suze's office, Kevin, Emily, and Jeff had joined them.

"What's it say? What's it say?" they all clamored.

Suze sat down and took out her letter opener.

"Oh, my God, you're so slow it's killing me," Meredith said.

Suze paused. "Okay, people. I appreciate your enthusiasm. But please realize that this is the second letter I've received. The first already informed me that I lost. This is probably another legal document, a coupon for a massage, or some other buy-off. Don't get your hopes up."

"Right," Meredith teased. "I saw how quickly you ended that meeting. But I'll be super careful not to get *my* hopes up."

"I'm not sure what I'm supposed to hope for," said Jeff.

"Ten million dollars!" said Emily.

"She already lost," Kevin, Meredith, and Jeff all said at the same time.

Suze smiled. "Glad we got that straightened out." She opened the envelope and pulled out a letter. There was a check attached to it, made out to her, in the amount of $250,000.

"Oh, my God, what? What is it? Did you win?" Meredith was hyperventilating.

"I see a check!" squealed Emily.

"Would this be an inappropriate time for me to say that I've always thought we had a bit of chemistry?" said Jeff, so quietly that none of them noticed.

"Shhh, guys, stop. I still didn't win," Suze said, scanning the note. "Nothing's changed. It's just that—I've been given a consolation prize. Wow. I don't know what to think."

"How much is it?" Kevin asked.

"It's…it's a lot," Suze said. She carefully put the check in her wallet.

"Oh, my God, that's better than winning. You get a sweet settlement, and you still get to go out and fall in love with anyone you want, rich or poor," said Meredith.

Suze's mind was still reeling. It was so much money. What had she done to deserve it? What did it mean to accept it?

But she thought of the California Schoolroom. This was it— her chance to make a private investment in a company that might change children's lives. It was as if fate had handed her the opportunity to invest in something she was truly passionate about. She smiled and turned to Meredith. "Can you see if those nonprofit guys already left the building? If they're still here, bring them back in."

CHAPTER 28

FOR THE SECOND day in a row there was a knock at the door during breakfast. This time Caroline was too slow on the draw, and her sister came running back to the table with a yellow envelope in hand.

"It's for you!" Brooke cried. "Maybe it's ten million dollars!"

"It's not," Caroline hissed, snatching the envelope away from her and trying to hide it in the newspaper. She was too late. Isabelle stopped making coffee, came over, and pulled the envelope out of its hiding place.

"What have we here?" she asked. "Go ahead and open it, sweetie, the suspense is killing me."

Caroline sighed. She already knew she'd lost, but what could she do? The slight stall was too much for Isabelle. She grabbed the envelope and tore it open. As she scanned it, a look of rapture crossed her face.

Caroline turned to Brooke. "Mom just found out she's a guest star on *Jay Leno's Garage*?"

Brooke took the bait. "She won a year's supply of energy supplements?"

Caroline said, "It's from Jesus Christ himself."

Brooke added, "Hence the messenger."

"Are you ladies quite done making fun of your poor old mother?" Isabelle asked. She handed the letter to Caroline. "Forgive me for caring."

Caroline recognized the letterhead on the note—a logo with the initials *GM*—it was the same as on the rejection note she'd received the day before. But to her surprise, this note politely requested her presence at the offices of Greenfield May. Why? What could this mean? She'd already been notified that Nicholas was not continuing the contest. She turned the paper over. The back was unsurprisingly blank. There was no other information.

Isabelle had no idea that Caroline had already received a letter informing her that the contest was over without a winner. Isabelle was about to explode with joy. She pulled Caroline out of her chair and, despite meeting complete resistance, tried to dance her around the kitchen. "You've done it! I'm so proud of you!"

"Mom—I don't think—"

"Greenfield May. You know who that is, don't you?" Isabelle screeched.

"As a matter of fact, I've never heard of them."

Isabelle squinted at Caroline. "When is the meeting? Let's see if Andre can squeeze you in for some highlights before then." She grabbed the bagel out of Caroline's hand. "And why don't you hold off on the carbs? I'll get you some celery. Two days *can* make a difference. It's all bloat, but who cares."

Caroline reread the letter. Why should she go to this meeting?

He'd already wasted her time, gotten her hopes up, and, perhaps worst of all, sent her mother down a rabbit hole of fantasy from which she might never return. Why hadn't this guy just asked a few girls out on dates? Maybe hired a top-notch matchmaker? Caroline was tired of all the over-the-top secrecy and maneuvering. She wanted to hock the diamond studs, find an apartment, and get back to her life.

But she had to go.

CHAPTER 29

THE OFFICES OF Greenfield May were in one of the new, hip seaside developments that were starting to take over Venice. As Caroline exited the elevator on the third floor, it occurred to her that her mother, who had reacted to the name of the business, had never explained what it was and why she was so excited by it. And Caroline had failed to google it. Her hand went to her pocket, toying with her phone. Now she was suddenly dying to google Greenfield May, but it was too late. Janey was already sitting in the lobby, gazing at a wall-sized aquarium, when Caroline arrived.

"Caroline, yay! These fish are supposed to make me calm, but I don't feel calm yet. I have to quit coffee, don't I? I don't know why I'm happy to see you—you're the competition. I think."

"All I can say is I have no idea what is going on," Caroline said. She also felt kind of glad to see a familiar face. Should she ask Janey if she'd also gotten a rejection letter before this meeting? What if Janey hadn't been rejected? What if Janey was here as the leading candidate and Caroline was something less? A backup. Heck, for all Caroline knew, Janey was another judge. In which case Caroline wanted to give her a piece of her mind. So she said, "Frankly, I'm kind of over this, and I don't care if he knows. He thinks we're at his beck and call. And he already sent me a letter telling me I wasn't the one."

"Me, too!" Janey said. "I actually had to plead my case to get this meeting."

"What did you do?" Caroline was impressed. If he wanted a go-getter, Janey was clearly his woman.

"I realized that at work I fight tooth and nail for projects I care about. I should devote the same effort to my love life, right? If it doesn't work out, well, I'm used to that. My shows get killed constantly. But I'd like to at least know I made my pitch."

Caroline felt an extra swell of nervousness. Should she be fighting tooth and nail for this? How could she fight for someone she'd never met? She envied Janey's conviction. "So what happens now?" Caroline asked.

"That's for him to know and us to find out," said Janey.

A door opened and out stepped a woman they both recognized, Alicia of the blue glasses.

"Hello, ladies. Nice to see you again. Janey, can you please come with me?"

"Wish me luck," Janey said with an exaggerated wink at Caroline.

"Sorry, can't do that," Caroline said, laughing. Janey disappeared into the office, and Caroline was left in the waiting room. For the first fifteen minutes she read the news on her phone, looking up with anticipation whenever she heard the faintest noise.

Then, as time went on, she got increasingly anxious. What did it mean that Janey had been called in first? Why was this taking so long? Janey must be doing well. Whose brilliant idea had it been to call both of them in at the same time? Maybe she should just give up and go home. After forty-five minutes she stopped caring whether she was being watched or might be busted and finally googled Greenfield May. She began to read the Wikipedia entry: *Greenfield May is an investment firm specializing in international*—

"Excuse me, Caroline? Are you ready?" Alicia had silently entered and was standing over her. Caroline fumbled to shut off the phone. Alicia led Caroline past the elevator bank, where Janey stood, tucking an envelope into her bag. Letting Alicia get a bit ahead, Caroline slowed down to whisper to Janey.

"Did you meet him?"

Janey nodded. "Ye—"

Before she could say more, Alicia gestured Caroline forward urgently. Janey whispered a quick "Good luck." Caroline hurried away, down the hall after Alicia. This was it. She was going to meet the mystery man at last.

CHAPTER 30

IT WAS NOT Nicholas. The rejection letter had been signed by Nicholas, but the man who stood up to shake her hand introduced himself as Tom Greenfield. He smiled nicely. That was what Caroline noticed first. He looked embarrassed and eager at the same time. He gestured for her to have a seat on the pale linen sofa. It was hard to take it all in. There was Tom, lean and handsome, with green eyes and a slant of dark hair, and the office, with its neutral tones and dramatic art, and the intrigue of the great Greenfield enterprises.

"Hi, Tom," she said, laughing and shaking her head. "I have a lot of questions for you."

He grinned sheepishly. "I'm sure you do. Fire away."

Tom, she was thinking. *This is the man I've been wondering about, and his name is Tom. He is still a total stranger, but now he has a name. Will it come to be familiar to me, so familiar that it seems there's always been Tom?*

"Are you definitely you? The mystery man? I mean, I got a letter from Nicholas, and there have been so many interviews that I just need to know—"

"You've reached the end of the line," Tom said. He smiled again, and Caroline's heart dipped a bit. "I'm it. I'm sorry for that letter. Those were my words, but I used Nicholas's name on your letter—and different names on the other letters—because I was counseled to keep my name out of all the correspondence. I know it sounds ridiculous. I mean, it *is* ridiculous! But as you might imagine, I have my own share of doubts about this process. Thank you for enduring all of it, for being here."

Caroline looked around. "I feel like I'm still being interviewed. See my perfect posture?"

"You're right. I'm an idiot. No, actually, I had to meet another candidate—"

"Janey," Caroline said.

"That's right, you two have met. I'm sorry about that, too. It must have been awkward," he said.

"It's okay, actually. We kind of became friends. At least I like your taste."

"But I did think—if it's okay with you—we could get out of here." He pointed out the window, which had an expansive view of the beach. "It's better over there."

Caroline smiled. Rich though he might be, he wasn't arrogant.

CHAPTER 31

VENICE BEACH WAS wide, a long trudge through sand from the footpath to the edge of the ocean. They were quiet as they walked, and Caroline wondered if they would find their footing once they literally found their footing. Close to the water they came to a vacant lifeguard station. It was picturesque; a rough wooden ramp led up to a platform, in the middle of which stood a tall lifeguard chair. Without needing to discuss it, they headed up the ramp, its surface a relief from the drag of the beach.

"Is this okay? I didn't plan this part," Tom said.

"Good," said Caroline. "Not planning is perfect, and this is perfect."

They sat at the edge of the platform, legs dangling off the side, arms hooked over the lowest rail.

"I believe in soul mates," Tom said. "But not just one. Think about it—all these people find true love, but how many potential mates do they encounter? A few hundred? A thousand?"

"Four?" Caroline suggested jokingly.

"There are no perfect mates, but there are hundreds of potential soul mates that you might never encounter. I believe love is hard to find but easy to recognize. So I tried to improve my chances. And here we are."

"Not to fish for compliments, but why me? Don't get me wrong, I like myself well enough. But I used to—well, my mother used to make me audition for tons of stuff, and I have a track record of not winning. I was never anyone's top choice."

Tom leaned toward her, nudging her a bit with his shoulder. "That. Your honesty. At least, that's part of it. This wasn't a game for you, something you wanted to win. To tell the truth, I actually liked that you applied because your mother insisted."

"It was for only five hundred dollars! See? I'm a cheap date!"

"And I might have thought your heart wasn't in it, but the more I learned about you, the more I thought that you were afraid to let yourself hope. That boyfriend who left you—"

Caroline covered her face. "Oh, my God, you really do know everything about me."

"We'll even the score, I promise," Tom said. A cool wind blew off the water, and Caroline pulled her hands into her sleeves for warmth. "I'm going to use that as an excuse to help you stay warm," Tom said, moving right next to her and putting an arm around her shoulders. "Is this okay?"

Caroline leaned into him. He was warm. It was more than okay.

"Speaking of soul mates—I think there might have been real chemistry between Suze and one of her interviewers," Caroline said.

"Oh, right!" Tom said, pulling his phone out of his pocket.

"Thanks for reminding me. I'm making a note to myself to put Miguel in touch with her."

Caroline smiled. That was the one. Miguel. There was hope for him and Suze yet.

Putting his phone away, Tom said, "I was right about you. The fact that you're thinking of the two of them and not yourself right now…I saw that generous spirit in your devotion to the kids you work with. Society has given up on them—too soon—and you haven't. You believe in people."

It's true, Caroline thought. "That's pretty fundamental to who I am," she said.

"And that's how I knew that underneath it all you were open to possibility. I wanted someone who was open to this process, open to new experiences, open to exploring the odd twists that life might offer."

"Someone willing to believe that love might be hiding behind door number three," Caroline added. She was impressed. Tom seemed to get her. It didn't feel like they'd just met. "It's just— you're so…accomplished. And, full disclosure, I'm temporarily living with my mother. And she, full disclosure, is a piece of work. I worry that I'm not as together—"

He put up a hand. "Not to interrupt, but I was briefed. World's Worst Mother-in-Law. You know what? I'm up for the challenge."

They both laughed.

"Think of it from my side," he said. "Am I really supposed to limit my dating pool to people who have gotten to a certain point in their lives? There are so many other factors to consider. And though I have this one part of my life squared away, it doesn't mean I have *everything* figured out. Even my house—I rent everything that's in it. I didn't want to furnish a house according to my taste and ask a woman to join me in it. I want to make a life with someone and build it from scratch. I want a partner."

Caroline chuckled. "I was a little put off by your rejection letter. And then you changed your mind so quickly. But now I see it's actually kind of a plus. I'm glad you aren't 100 percent confident in this strange method of yours—or in yourself."

"See? I'm still a work in progress."

Tom wasn't at all what Caroline had expected. He didn't seem like a high-powered businessman. He wasn't checking her qualities off on a list or impatient to seal the deal with her. And then there was the matter of how close he was sitting to her. She was hyper-aware of every point where their bodies were touching. It made her shiver, and the more she shivered, the tighter he held her.

"You said you believe in more than one soul mate," she said. "It sounds like you've been in love before."

"Yes," he said, and as she watched, a riddle of emotions passed over his face. Was he about to laugh or cry? He took a deep breath and said, "About ten years ago, when I was in my late twenties, I lost someone I loved. After that I started this company and put everything I had into it. All my time, all my energy. I couldn't replace her, so I worked my ass off instead."

"If your success is a measure of your grief, then you must have missed her a whole lot," Caroline said with all the sympathy that she felt.

"I'm proud of what I've done, and it brings me joy to succeed. But I've always felt that the most meaningful accomplishment in my life was loving Mary."

He was matter-of-fact—Caroline could see that although he had obviously been greatly affected by this woman's death, it had been a full decade. He had recovered as much as he ever would. And yet his enduring love for her, and respect for the value of that love, was moving.

"I haven't been a total hermit. I've tried to date. But it never seemed to work out. Maybe someone else could appreciate this kind of success by himself, without a partner, but that's not how I'm wired. Love is the most important part of life."

They had been looking out at the water, but now Caroline put her hand on his and turned to face him.

"Thank you for telling me that," she said. And for a moment they just looked at each other, feeling strange but comfortable, unknown but known, unsure but hopeful. When Tom spoke, his voice was quiet and serious.

"This ten-million-dollar thing was a crazy scheme. But there was always a possibility that it could work, that I would meet the right woman. And if it worked, it would all be worth it. So that brings the two of us to the present, right here, right now."

CHAPTER 32

CAROLINE FELT DIZZY. What was happening to her? She didn't believe in love at first sight, but the world seemed to be spinning a little faster than usual.

"I need to stand up," she said. "Can we walk?"

"Of course," Tom said, jumping to his feet and helping her up. "I know this is a lot...."

Side by side, they walked along the shoreline. It was a clear day, as always, and the low tide left the sand at the water's edge flat and easy to walk on. Tom held Caroline's hand, and it felt like the most natural thing in the world.

"You said if there was a *possibility* you could find the right person...." Caroline knew her way around an audition, but she had no idea where she stood with this still mostly mysterious man.

"That's right," he said softly. "Caroline, I liked you before I met you. But being with you is better. It feels easy. I'm sure it's not the same for you...not yet...but I think we have a shot at happiness, and that's all I was looking for. You are the winner. The ten million dollars is all yours."

"But…," Caroline gasped. What was happening? Now that it came down to it, she didn't believe this contest was actually real. It couldn't be true, that he was actually going to give her ten million dollars. It was incomprehensible. For all the auditions she'd failed, the parts she'd lost, the contests she'd never won, it couldn't be that her life was a fairy tale after all. And yet—she hadn't auditioned. She hadn't played a role. She had just been herself, the whole way through. She had never pretended to be perfect, or even much of a catch. She'd been honest every step of the way. If he liked her for who she really was, that changed everything.

And then—Tom knelt down next to her.

"No!" Caroline exclaimed.

"Don't worry," he said. "Please just hear me out." He took both her hands in his. "I realize we just met, so you don't know me, but I know you. You are funny, and kind to your sister, and tolerant of your mother. But what draws me to you most is something bigger than a witty answer in a questionnaire or a heartfelt conversation with a likeable interviewer. It's the way you see the world. I trust you implicitly. If there's anyone I would trust to make all my decisions going forward, it would be you."

"Me? I have no idea—"

"Being with you feels right. To be honest, it's hard not to take you in my arms. I know you're a step behind in knowing me, so I'm trying desperately not to move too fast."

Caroline blushed. She felt more ready to be taken in his arms than she was willing to admit. She knelt down in the sand so that she could see him face-to-face.

Tom squeezed her hands tightly. "I see your heart," Tom said. "Your heart has a very good sense of direction. I hope it comes my way. That is to say…" He paused and looked right into Caroline's eyes. "Will you marry me?" But before Caroline could speak, he held up a hand, stopping her. "Don't answer. Yet. This is just a proposal. For now, I hope we can get to know each other. I'll wait as long as you think we need. When you know me, when your heart guides you, then you can decide whether to accept the proposal. That's up to you."

"Oh, phew," Caroline said. "Because, well, this is a lot to process all at once. I feel…excited, scared…confused. I can't believe this is happening."

"I know," Tom said. "We have plenty of time. And just to be clear: the money is yours no matter what."

CHAPTER 33

CAROLINE LOOKED AROUND a bit unsteadily. The man in front of her had been a complete stranger a couple of hours ago, and now there was so much at stake. Prince Charming had asked for her hand in marriage. This was her mother's dream come true—but was it hers?

"So I can leave right now, right?" she said. "I can just walk back to my car with the money, if I even decide to accept it."

Tom's face changed. It was subtle, just a shadow of sadness or disappointment in his eyes, but he nodded and gave a small smile. "Of course," he said. "Well, not exactly with the cash. We'll have to wire the money into your account or something. Trust me, I'm good for it." He rose to his feet and stepped back to give her space.

Caroline moved toward him. She got closer. Closer. Then she held his face in her hands and looked into his eyes. Now there was a twinkle in them as he appreciated her unabashed appraisal. She liked his eyes.

"Here's to possibilities," she said. And then she kissed him.

CHAPTER 35

Someone wants to make his first big case his last

STORIES AT THE SPEED OF LIFE

JAMES
PATTERSON
BOOK**SHOTS**

FRENCH
KISS

DETECTIVE LUC MONCRIEF'S
FIRST BIG CASE
COULD BE HIS LAST

with RICHARD DILALLO

Read on for an extract

THE WEATHERMAN NAILED IT. "Sticky, hot, and miserable. Highs in the nineties. Stay inside if you can."

I can't. I have to get someplace. Fast.

Jesus Christ, it's hot. Especially if you're running as fast as you can through Central Park *and* you're wearing a dark gray Armani silk suit, a light gray Canali silk shirt, and black Ferragamo shoes.

As you might have guessed, I am late—very, very late. *Très en retard,* as we say in France.

I pick up speed until my legs hurt. I can feel little blisters forming on my toes and heels.

Why did I ever come to New York?

Why, oh why, did I leave Paris?

If I were running like this in Paris, I would be stopping all traffic. I would be the center of attention. Men and women would be shouting for the police.

"A young businessman has gone berserk! He is shoving baby carriages out of his path. He is frightening the old ladies walking their dogs."

But this is not Paris. This is New York.

So forget it. Even the craziest event in New York goes unnoticed. The dog walkers keep on walking their dogs. The teenage lovers kiss. A toddler points to me. His mother glances up. Then she shrugs.

Will even one New Yorker dial 911? Or 311?

Forget about that also. You see, I am part of the police. A French detective now working with the Seventeenth Precinct on my specialty—drug smuggling, drug sales, and drug-related homicides.

My talent for being late has, in a mere two months, become almost legendary with my colleagues in the precinct house. But… oh, *merde*…showing up late for today's meticulously planned stakeout on Madison Avenue and 71st Street will do nothing to help my reputation, a reputation as an uncooperative rich French kid, a rebel with too many causes.

Merde…today of all days I should have known better than to wake my gorgeous girlfriend to say good-bye.

"I cannot be late for this one, Dalia."

"Just one more good-bye squeeze. What if you're shot and I never see you again?"

The good-bye "squeeze" turned out to be significantly longer than I had planned.

Eh. It doesn't matter. I'm where I'm supposed to be now. A mere forty-five minutes late.

MY PARTNER, DETECTIVE Maria Martinez, is seated on the driver's side of an unmarked police car at 71st Street and Madison Avenue.

While keeping her eyes on the surrounding area, Maria unlocks the passenger door. I slide in, drowning in perspiration. She glances at me for a second, then speaks.

"Man. What's the deal? Did you put your suit on first and *then* take your shower?"

"Funny," I say. "Sorry I'm late."

"You should have little business cards with that phrase on it— 'Sorry I'm late.'"

I'm certain that Maria Martinez doesn't care whether I'm late. Unlike a lot of my detective colleagues, she doesn't mind that I'm not big on "protocol." I'm late a lot. I do a lot of careless things. I bring ammo for a Glock 22 when I'm packing a Glock 27. I like a glass or two of white wine with lunch…it's a long list. But Maria overlooks most of it.

My other idiosyncrasies she has come to accept, more or less. I must have a proper *déjeuner*. That's lunch. No mere sandwich will do. What's more, a glass or two of good wine never did anything but enhance the flavor of a lunch.

You see, Maria "gets" me. Even better, she knows what I know:

together we're a cool combination of her procedure-driven methods and my purely instinct-driven methods.

"So where are we with this bust?" I say.

"We're still sitting on our butts. That's where we are," she says.
Then she gives details.

"They got two pairs of cops on the other side of the street, and
two other detectives—Imani Williams and Henry Whatever-the-
Hell-His-Long-Polish-Name-Is—at the end of the block. That
team'll go into the garage.

"Then there's another team behind the garage. They'll hold
back and *then* go into the garage.

"Then they got three guys on the roof of the target building."

The target building is a large former town house that's now
home to a store called Taylor Antiquities. It's a place filled with the
fancy antique pieces lusted after by trust-fund babies and hedge-
fund hotshots. Maria and I have already cased Taylor Antiquities
a few times. It's a store where you can lay down your Amex Cen-
turion card and walk away with a white jade vase from the Yuan
dynasty or purchase the four-poster bed where John and Abigail
Adams reportedly conceived little John Quincy.

"And what about us?"

"Our assignment spot is inside the store," she says.

"No. I want to be where the action is," I say.

"Be careful what you wish for," Maria says. "Do what they tell
you. We're inside the store. Over and out. Meanwhile, how about
watching the street with me?"

Maria Martinez is total cop. At the moment she is heart-and-soul into the surveillance. Her eyes dart from the east side of the street to the west. Every few seconds, she glances into the rearview mirror. Follows it with a quick look into the side-view mirror. Searches straight ahead. Then she does it all over again.

Me? Well, I'm looking around, but I'm also wondering if I can take a minute off to grab a cardboard cup of lousy American coffee.

Don't get me wrong. And don't be put off by what I said about my impatience with "procedure." No. I am very cool with being a detective. In fact, I've wanted to be a detective since I was four years old. I'm also very good at my job. And I've got the résumé to prove it.

Last year in Pigalle, one of the roughest parts of Paris, I solved a drug-related gang homicide and made three on-the-scene arrests. Just me and a twenty-five-year-old traffic cop.

I was happy. I was successful. For a few days I was even famous.

The next morning the name Luc Moncrief was all over the newspapers and the Internet. A rough translation of the headline on the front page of *Le Monde*:

OLDEST PIGALLE DRUG GANG SMASHED BY YOUNGEST PARIS DETECTIVE— LUC MONCRIEF

Underneath was this subhead:

Parisian Heartthrob Hauls in Pigalle Drug Lords

The paparazzi had always been somewhat interested in whom I was dating; after that, they were obsessed. Club owners comped my table with bottles of Perrier-Jouët Champagne. Even my father, the chairman of a giant pharmaceuticals company, gave me one of his rare compliments.

"Very nice job…for a playboy. Now I hope you've got this 'detective thing' out of your system."

I told him thank you, but I did not tell him that "this detective thing" was not out of my system. Or that I enjoyed the very generous monthly allowance that he gave me too much.

So when my *capitaine supérieur* announced that the NYPD wanted to trade one of their art-forgery detectives for one of our Paris drug enforcement detectives for a few months, I jumped at the offer. From my point of view, it was a chance to reconnect with my former lover, Dalia Boaz. From my Parisian *lieutenant* point of view, it was an opportunity to add some needed discipline and learning to my instinctive approach to detective work.

So here I am. On Madison Avenue, my eyes are burning with sweat. I can actually feel the perspiration squishing around in my shoes.

Detective Martinez remains focused completely on the street scene. But God, I need some coffee, some air. I begin speaking.

"Listen. If I could just jump out for a minute and—"

As I'm about to finish the sentence, two vans—one black, one red—turn into the garage next door to Taylor Antiquities.

Our cell phones automatically buzz with a loud sirenlike sound. The doors of the unmarked police cars begin to open.

As Maria and I hit the street, she speaks.

"It looks like our evidence has finally arrived."

MARTINEZ AND I RUSH into Taylor Antiquities. There are no customers. A skinny middle-aged guy sits at a desk in the rear of the store, and a typical debutante—a young blond woman in a white linen skirt and a black shirt—is dusting some small, silver-topped jars.

It is immediately clear to both of them that we're not here to buy an ancient Thai penholder. We are easily identified as two very unpleasant-looking cops, the male foolishly dressed in an expensive waterlogged suit, the woman in too-tight khaki pants. Maria and I are each holding our NYPD IDs in our left hands and our pistols in our right hands.

"You. Freeze!" Maria shouts at the blond woman.

I yell the same thing at the guy at the desk.

"You freeze, too, sir," I say.

From our two pre-bust surveillance visits I recognize the man as Blaise Ansel, the owner of Taylor Antiquities.

Ansel begins walking toward us.

I yell again. "I said freeze, Mr. Ansel. This…is…a…drug… raid."

"This is police-department madness," Ansel says, and now he is almost next to us. The debutante hasn't moved a muscle.

"Cuff him, Luc. He's resisting." Maria is pissed.

Ansel throws his hands into the air. "No. No. I am not resisting anything but the intrusion. I *am* freezing. Look."

Although I have seen him before, I have never heard him speak. His accent is foreign, thick. It's an accent that's easy for anyone to identify. Ansel is a Frenchman. Son of a bitch. One of ours.

As Ansel freezes, three patrol cars, lights flashing, pull up in front of the store. Then I tell the young woman to join us. She doesn't move. She doesn't speak.

"Please join us," Maria says. Now the woman moves to us. Slowly. Cautiously.

"Your name, ma'am?" I ask.

"Monica Ansel," she replies.

Blaise Ansel looks at Martinez and me.

"She's my wife."

There's got to be a twenty-year age difference between the two of them, but Maria and I remain stone-faced. Maria taps on her cell phone and begins reading aloud from the screen.

"To make this clear: we are conducting a drug search based on probable cause. Premises and connected premises are 861 Madison Avenue, New York, New York, in the borough of Manhattan, June 21, 2016. Premises title: Taylor Antiquities, Inc. Chairman and owner: Blaise Martin Ansel. Company president: Blaise Martin Ansel."

Maria taps the screen and pushes another button.

"This is being recorded," she says.

I would never have read the order to search, but Maria is strictly by the book.

"This is preposterous," says Blaise Ansel.

Maria does not address Ansel's comment. She simply says, "I want you to know that detectives and officers are currently positioned in your delivery dock, your garage, and your rooftop. They will be interviewing all parties of interest. It is our assignment to interview both you and the woman you've identified as your wife."

"Drugs? Are you mad?" yells Ansel. "This shop is a museum-quality repository of rare antiques. Look. Look."

Ansel quickly moves to one of the display tables. He holds up a carved mahogany box. "A fifteenth-century tea chest," he says. He lifts the lid of the box. "What do you see inside? Cocaine? Heroin? Marijuana?"

It is obvious that Maria has decided to allow Ansel to continue his slightly crazed demonstration.

"This—this, too," Ansel says as he moves to a pine trunk set on four spindly legs. "An American colonial sugar safe. Nothing inside. No crystal meth, no sugar."

Ansel is about to present two painted Chinese-looking bowls when the rear entrance to the shop opens and Imani Williams enters. Detective Williams is agitated. She is also *très belle*.

"Not a damn thing in those two vans," she says. "Police mechanics are searching the undersides, but there's nothing but a bunch of empty gold cigarette boxes and twelve Iranian silk rugs in the cargo. We tested for drug traces. They all came up negative."

I think I catch an exchange of glances between Monsieur and

Madame Ansel. I *think*. I'm not sure. But the more I think, well, the more sure I become.

"Detective Williams," I say. "Do you think you could fill in for me for a few minutes to assist Detective Martinez with the Ansel interview?"

"Yeah, sure," says Williams. "Where you going?"

"I just need to…I'm not sure…look around."

"Tell the truth, Moncrief. You've been craving a cup of joe since you got here," says Maria Martinez.

"Can't fool you, partner," I say.

I open the shop door. I'm out.

THE SUFFOCATING AIR ON Madison Avenue almost shimmers with heat.

Where have all the beautiful people gone? East Hampton? Bar Harbor? The South of France?

I walk the block. I watch a man polish the handrail alongside the steps of Saint James' Church. I see the tourists line up outside Ladurée, the French *macaron* store.

A young African American man, maybe eighteen years old, walks near me. He is bare-chested. He seems even sweatier than I am. The young man's T-shirt is tied around his neck, and he is guzzling from a quart-size bottle of water.

"Where'd you get that?" I ask.

"A dude like you can go to that fancy-ass cookie store. You got five bills, that'll get you a soda there," he says.

"But where'd you get *that* bottle, the water you're drinking?" I ask again.

"Us poor bros go to Kenny's. You're practically in it right now."

He gestures toward 71st Street between Madison and Park Avenues. As the kid moves away, I figure that the "fancy-ass cookie store" is Ladurée. I am equidistant between a five-dollar soda and a cheaper but larger bottle of water. Why waste Papa's generous allowance on fancy-ass soda?

Kenny's is a tiny storefront, a place you should find closer to Ninth Avenue than Madison Avenue. Behind the counter is a Middle Eastern-type guy. Kenny? He peddles only newspapers, cigarettes, lottery tickets, and, for some reason, Dial soap.

I examine the contents of Kenny's small refrigerated case. It holds many bottles, all of them the same—the no-name water that the shirtless young man was drinking. At the moment that water looks to me like heaven in a bottle.

"I'm going to take two of these bottles," I say.

"One second, please, sir," says the man behind the counter, then he addresses another man who is wheeling four brown cartons of candy into the store. The cartons are printed with the name and logo for Snickers. The man steering the dolly looks very much like the counterman. Is he Kenny? Is anybody Kenny? I consider buying a Snickers bar. No. The wet Armani suit is already growing tighter.

"How many more boxes are there, Hector?" the counterman asks.

"At least fifteen more," comes the response. Then "Kenny" turns to me.

"And you, sir?" the counterman asks.

"No. Nothing," I say. "Sorry."

I leave the tiny store and break into a run. I am around the corner on Madison Avenue. I punch the button on my phone marked 4. Direct connection to Martinez. All I can think is: *What the*

*hell? Twenty cartons of candy stored in a shop the size of a closet?
Twenty cartons of Snickers in a store that doesn't even sell candy?*

She answers and starts talking immediately. "Williams and I are
getting nowhere with these two assholes. This whole thing sucks.
Our intelligence is all screwed up. There's nothing here."

I am only slightly breathless, only slightly nervous.

"Listen to me. It's all here, where I am. I know it."

"What the hell are you talking about?" she says.

"A newsstand between Madison and Park. Kenny's. I'm less
than two hundred feet away from you guys. Leave one person at
Taylor Antiquities and get everyone over here. Now."

"How—?"

"The two vans, the garage…that's all a decoy," I say. "The real
shit is being unloaded here…in cartons of candy bars."

"How do you know?"

"Like the case in Pigalle. *I know because I know.*"

ONE MONTH LATER. IT'S another sweltering summer day in Manhattan.

A year ago I was working in the detective room at the precinct on rue Achille-Martinet in Paris. Today I'm working in the detective room at the precinct on East 51st Street in Manhattan.

But the crime is absolutely the same. In both cities, men, women, and children sell drugs, kill for drugs, and all too often die for drugs.

My desk faces Maria Martinez's scruffy desk. She's not in yet. Uh-oh. She may be picking up my bad habits. *Pas possible.* Not Maria.

I drink my coffee and begin reading the blotter reports of last night's arrests. No murders, no drug busts. So much for interesting blotter reports.

I call my coolest, hippest, chicest New York contact—Patrick, one of the doormen at 15 Central Park West, where I live with Dalia. Patrick is trying to score me a dinner reservation at Rao's, the impossible-to-get-into restaurant in East Harlem.

Merde. I am on my cell phone when my boss, Inspector Nick Elliott, the chief inspector for my division, stops by. I hold up my "just a minute" index finger. Since the Taylor Antiquities drug bust I have a little money in the bank with my boss, but it won't last forever, and this hand gesture certainly won't help.

At last I sigh. No tables. Maybe next month. When I hang up the phone I say, "I'm sorry, Inspector. I was just negotiating a favor with a friend who might be able to score me a table at Rao's next week."

Elliott scowls and says, "Far be it from me to interrupt your off-duty life, Moncrief, but you may have noticed that your partner isn't at her desk."

"I noticed. Don't forget, I'm a detective."

He ignores my little joke.

"In case you're wondering, Detective Martinez is on loan to Vice for two days."

"Why didn't you or Detective Martinez tell me this earlier? You must have known before today."

"Yeah, I knew about it yesterday, but I told Martinez to hold off telling you. That it would just piss you off to be left out, and I was in no rush to listen to you get pissed off," Elliott says.

"So why *wasn't* I included?" I ask.

"You weren't necessary. They just needed a woman. Though I don't owe you any explanations about assignments."

The detective room has grown quieter. I'm sure that a few of my colleagues—especially the men—are enjoying seeing Elliott put me in my place.

Fact is, I like Elliott; he's a pretty straight-arrow guy, but I have been developing a small case of paranoia about being excluded from hot assignments.

"What can Maria do that I can't do?" I ask.

"If you can't answer that, then that pretty-boy face of yours isn't doing you much good," Elliott says with a laugh. Then his tone of voice turns serious.

"Anyway, we got something going on up the road a piece. They got a situation at Brioni. That's a fancy men's store just off Fifth Avenue. Get a squad car driver to take you there. Right now."

"Which Brioni?" I ask.

"I just told you—Brioni on Fifth Avenue."

"There are *two* Brionis: 57 East 57th Street and 55 East 52nd Street," I say.

Elliott begins to walk away. He stops. He turns to me. He speaks.

"You *would* know something like that."

JAMES PATTERSON
BOOK**SHOTS**

OUT THIS MONTH

FRENCH KISS

French detective Luc Moncrief joined the NYPD for a fresh start – but someone wants to make his first big case his last.

$10,000,000 MARRIAGE PROPOSAL

A billboard offering $10 million to get married intrigues three single women in LA. But who is Mr. Right... and is he the perfect match for the lucky winner?

SACKING THE QUARTERBACK

Attorney Melissa St. James wins every case. Now, when she's up against American football superstar Grayson Knight, her heart is on the line, too.

KILL OR BE KILLED

Four gripping thrillers – one killer collection. *The Trial*, *Little Black Dress*, *Heist* and *The Women's War*.

THE WOMEN'S WAR (ebook only)

Former Marine Corps colonel Amanda Collins and her lethal team of women warriors have vowed to avenge her family's murder.

THE RETURN (ebook only)

When an accident brings her high-school sweetheart back home to recover, Ashley's determined to avoid him. But can she stop herself from falling into his embrace?

JAMES PATTERSON
BOOK**SHOTS**
COMING SOON

KILLER CHEF

Someone is poisoning the diners in New Orleans' best restaurants.
Now it's up to chef and homicide cop Caleb Rooney to catch
a killer set on revenge.

DAZZLING: THE DIAMOND TRILOGY, PART 1

To support her artistic career, Siobhan Dempsey works at the elite
Stone Room in New York City... never expecting to be swept away by
tech billionaire Derick Miller.

BODYGUARD

Special Agent Abbie Whitmore has only one task: protect
Congressman Jonathan Lassiter from a violent cartel's threats.
Yet she's never had to do it while falling in love...

BOOK**SHOTS**

STORIES AT THE SPEED OF LIFE

www.bookshots.com

ALSO BY JAMES PATTERSON

Private Vegas (*with Maxine Paetro*)
Private Sydney (*with Kathryn Fox*)
Private Paris (*with Mark Sullivan*)
The Games (*with Mark Sullivan*)

NYPD RED SERIES

NYPD Red (*with Marshall Karp*)
NYPD Red 2 (*with Marshall Karp*)
NYPD Red 3 (*with Marshall Karp*)
NYPD Red 4 (*with Marshall Karp*)

STAND-ALONE THRILLERS

Sail (*with Howard Roughan*)
Swimsuit (*with Maxine Paetro*)
Don't Blink (*with Howard Roughan*)
Postcard Killers (*with Liza Marklund*)
Toys (*with Neil McMahon*)
Now You See Her (*with Michael Ledwidge*)
Kill Me If You Can (*with Marshall Karp*)
Guilty Wives (*with David Ellis*)
Zoo (*with Michael Ledwidge*)
Second Honeymoon (*with Howard Roughan*)
Mistress (*with David Ellis*)
Invisible (*with David Ellis*)
The Thomas Berryman Number
Truth or Die (*with Howard Roughan*)
Murder House (*with David Ellis*)
Never Never (*with Candice Fox*)
Woman of God (*with Maxine Paetro*)

NON-FICTION

Torn Apart (*with Hal and Cory Friedman*)

The Murder of King Tut (*with Martin Dugard*)

ROMANCE

Sundays at Tiffany's (*with Gabrielle Charbonnet*)
The Christmas Wedding (*with Richard DiLallo*)
First Love (*with Emily Raymond*)

OTHER TITLES

Miracle at Augusta (*with Peter de Jonge*)

BOOKSHOTS

Black & Blue (*with Candice Fox*)
Break Point (*with Lee Stone*)
Cross Kill
Private Royals (*with Rees Jones*)
The Hostage (*with Robert Gold*)
Zoo 2 (*with Max DiLallo*)
Heist (*with Rees Jones*)
Hunted (*with Andrew Holmes*)
Airport: Code Red (*with Michael White*)
The Trial (*with Maxine Paetro*)
Little Black Dress (*with Emily Raymond*)
Chase (*with Michael Ledwidge*)
Let's Play Make-Believe (*with James O. Born*)
Dead Heat (*with Lee Stone*)
Triple Threat
113 Minutes (*with Max DiLallo*)
The Verdict (*with Robert Gold*)